“Miss Sloane, I think you misunderstand something about what’s going on here.”

Sheridan’s heart skipped. Why was Rashid so beautiful? And why was he such a contrast? He was fire and ice in one person. Hot eyes, cold heart. It almost made her sad. But why should it? She did not know him, and what she did know so far hadn’t endeared him to her. “Do I?”

“Indeed. I am not Mr. Rashid.”

“Then who are you?”

He looked haughty, and her stomach threatened to heave again. Because there was something familiar about that face, she realized. She’d seen it on the news a few weeks ago.

He spoke, his voice clear and firm and lightly accented. “I am King Rashid bin Zaid al-Hassan, the Great Protector of my people, the Lion of Kyr, and Defender of the Throne. And you, Miss Sloane, may be carrying my heir.”

Heirs to the Throne of Kyr

Two brothers, one crown and a royal duty that cannot be denied...

The desert kingdom of Kyr needs a new ruler.

Prince Kadir al-Hassan, the Eagle of Kyr:
The world's most notorious playboy.

Prince Rashid al-Hassan, the Lion of Kyr:
As dark-hearted as the desert itself.

These sheikh princes share the same blood, but they couldn't be more different. So now there's only one question on everyone's lips....

Who will be crowned the new desert king?

Don't miss this thrilling new duet from Lynn Raye Harris—where duty and desire collide against a sizzling desert landscape!

Gambling with the Crown

May 2014

Carrying the Sheikh's Heir

July 2014

Lynn Raye Harris

Carrying the Sheikh's Heir

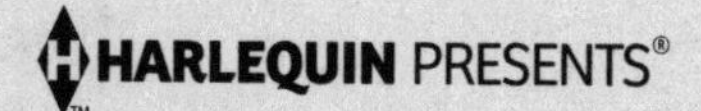

Recycling programs for this product may not exist in your area.

ISBN-13: 978-0-373-13257-7

CARRYING THE SHEIKH'S HEIR

First North American Publication 2014

This edition published by arrangement with Harlequin Books S.A.

For questions and comments about the quality of this book, please contact us at CustomerService@Harlequin.com.

Printed in U.S.A.

All about the author...
Lynn Raye Harris

USA TODAY bestselling author **LYNN RAYE HARRIS** burst onto the scene when she won a writing contest held by Harlequin. The prize was an editor for a year—but only six months later, Lynn sold her first novel. A former finalist for the Romance Writers of America's Golden Heart Award, Lynn lives in Alabama with her handsome husband and two crazy cats. Her stories have been called "exceptional and emotional," "intense," and "sizzling." You can visit her at www.lynnrayeharris.com.

Other titles by Lynn Raye Harris available in ebook:

GAMBLING WITH THE CROWN *(Heirs to the Throne of Kyr)*
THE CHANGE IN DI NAVARRA'S PLAN
A FAÇADE TO SHATTER *(Sicily's Corretti Dynasty)*
A GAME WITH ONE WINNER *(Scandal in the Spotlight)*

To my brainstorming partners, Jean Hovey and Stephanie Jones, who write together as Alicia Hunter Pace. They calmly listen to my ideas, toss out helpful suggestions, and don't get offended when I don't use a single one. And when I tell them there might be jackals, they reply that you can never have too many jackals.
Thanks for having my back, ladies.

CHAPTER ONE

"A MISTAKE? How is this possible?"

King Rashid bin Zaid al-Hassan glared daggers at the stuttering secretary who stood in front of him. The man swallowed visibly.

"The clinic says they have made a mistake, Your Majesty. A woman..." Mostafa looked down at the note in his hand. "A woman in America was supposed to receive her brother-in-law's sperm. She received yours instead."

Rashid's blood ran hot and then cold. He felt... violated. Rage coursed through him like a flame from a blast furnace, melting the ice around his heart for only a moment before it hardened again. He knew from experience that nothing could thaw that ice for long. In five years, nothing had penetrated the darkness surrounding him.

His hands clenched into fists on his desk. This was too much. Too outrageous.

How dare they? How dare anyone take that choice away from him? He wasn't ready for a child in his life. He didn't know if he would ever be ready, though eventually he had to provide Kyr with an heir. It was his duty, but he wasn't prepared to do it quite yet.

The prospect of marrying and producing children

brought up too many memories, too much pain. He preferred the ice to the sharpness of loss and despair that would envelop him if he let the ice thaw.

He'd obeyed the law that required him to deposit sperm in two banks for the preservation of his line, but he'd never dreamed it could go so horribly wrong. A random woman had been impregnated with his sperm. He could even now be an expectant father, his seed growing into a tiny life that could break him anew.

An icy wash of terror crested inside him, left him reeling in its wake. He would be physically ill in another moment.

Rashid pushed himself up from his chair and turned away so Mostafa wouldn't see the utter desolation that he knew was on his face. This was not an auspicious beginning to his reign as Kyr's king.

Hell, as if this was the only thing that had gone wrong. His stomach churned with fresh fury.

Since his father died two months ago and his brother abdicated before he'd ever been crowned, it was now Rashid's duty to rule this nation. But nothing was the way it was supposed to be. As the eldest, he should have been the crown prince, but he'd been the despised son, a pawn in his father's game of cat and mouse. In Kyr, the king could name his successor from amongst his sons. There was no law that said it had to be the eldest, though tradition usually dictated that it was.

But not for King Zaid al-Hassan. He'd been a cruel and manipulative man, the kind who ruled his sons—and his wives—with fear and harsh punishments. He'd dangled the possibility of the throne over his sons' heads for far too long. Kadir had never wanted to rule, but it hadn't mattered to their father. It was simply a way to control his eldest son. But Rashid had refused to play, instead leaving Kyr when he was twenty-five and vowing never to come back again.

He had come back, however. And now he wore a crown he'd never expected to have. His father, the old snake, was probably spinning in his grave right this minute. King Zaid had not wanted Rashid to rule. He had only wanted to hold out the hope of it before snatching the crown away in a final act of spite. That he'd died without naming his successor didn't fill Rashid with the kind of peace that Kadir felt. Kadir wanted to believe their father had desired a reconciliation, and Rashid would not take that away from him.

But Rashid knew better. He'd had a lifetime of his father's scorn and disapproval and he just simply knew better.

Yet here he was. Rashid's gaze scanned the desert landscape, rolling over the sandstone hills in the distance, the red sand dunes, the palms and fountains that lined the ornate gardens of the palace. The sun was high and most people were inside at this hour. The horizon shimmered with heat. A primitive satisfaction rolled through him at the sight of all he loved.

He'd missed Kyr. He'd missed her perfumed night breezes, her blazing heat and her hardy people. He'd missed the call to prayer ringing from the mosque in the dawn hour, and he'd missed riding across the desert on his Arabian stallion, a hawk on his arm, hunting the small animals that were the hawk's chosen prey.

Until two months ago, he'd not set foot in Kyr in ten years. He'd thought he never would again, but then his father had called with news of his illness and demanded

Rashid's presence. Even then, Rashid had resisted. For Kadir's sake, he had finally relented.

And now he was a king when he'd given up on the idea years ago. Kadir was gone again, married to his former personal assistant and giddy with love. For Kadir, the world was a bright, happy place filled with possibilities.

Desolation swept through Rashid. It was an old and familiar companion, and his hands clenched into helpless fists. He'd been in love once and he'd been happy. But happiness was ephemeral and love didn't last. Love meant loss, and loss meant pain that never healed.

He'd been powerless to save Daria and the baby. So powerless. Who knew such a thing was possible in this day and age? A woman dying in childbirth seemed impossible, and yet it was not. It was, in fact, ridiculously easy. Rashid knew it far too well.

He stood there awhile longer, facing the windswept dunes in the distance, gathering his thoughts before he turned back to his secretary. His voice, when he spoke, was dangerously measured. He would *not* let this thing rule him.

"We chose this facility in Atlanta as the repository of the second sample for a reason. You will call them and demand to know this woman's name and where she lives. Or they will suffer the very public consequences of their mistake."

Mostafa bowed his head. "Yes, Your Majesty." He sank to his knees then and touched his forehead to the ornate carpet that graced the floor in front of Rashid's desk. "It is my fault, Your Majesty. I chose the facility. I will resign my position and leave the capital in disgrace."

Rashid gritted his teeth. Sometimes he forgot how

rigidly prideful Kyrians could be. He'd spent so many years away. But if he'd stayed, he would be a different man. A less damaged man. Or not. His mother and father had been willing to use any weapon in their protracted war against each other, and he had been the favorite. The damage had been done years before he'd ever left Kyr.

"You will do no such thing," he snapped. "I have no time to wait while you train a new secretary. The fault lies elsewhere."

Rashid stalked back to his desk and sat down again. He had many things to do and a new problem to deal with. If this American woman had truly been impregnated with his sperm, then she could very well be carrying the heir to the throne of Kyr.

His fingers tightened on the pen he'd picked up again. If he thought of the child that way, as his heir, and of the woman as a functionary performing a duty—or a vessel carrying a cargo—then he could get through these next few days. Beyond that, he did not know.

An image of Daria's pale face swam in his head, twisting the knife deep in his soul. He was not ready to do this again, to watch a woman grow big with his child and know that it could all go wrong in an instant.

And yet he had no choice. If the woman was pregnant, she was his.

"Find this woman by the end of the hour," he ordered. "Or you may yet find yourself tending camels in the Kyrian Waste."

Mostafa's color drained as he backed away. "Yes, Your Majesty."

There was a snapping sound at precisely the moment the door closed behind the secretary. Pain bloomed in Rashid's palm. He looked down to find a pen in his hand.

Or, rather, half a pen. The other half lay on the desk, dark ink spilling into a pattern on the wood like a psychologist's test blot.

A cut in his skin dripped red blood onto the black ink. He watched it drip for a long moment before there was a knock on his door and a servant entered with afternoon tea. Rashid stood and went into the nearby restroom in order to wash away the blood and tape up the cut. When he returned to his desk, the blood and ink had been wiped away. Cleaned up as if it had never happened.

He flexed his hand and felt the sting of the cut against his palm. You could sweep up messes, patch up wounds and try to forget they ever happened.

But Rashid knew the truth. The cut would heal, but there were things that never went away, no matter how deeply you buried them.

"Please stop crying, Annie." Sheridan sat at her desk with her phone to her ear and her heart in her throat. Her sister was sobbing on the other end of the line at the news from the clinic. Sheridan was still too stunned to process it. "We'll get through this. Somehow, we'll get through. I *am* having a baby for you. I promise it will happen."

Annie sobbed and wailed for twenty minutes while Sheridan tried to soothe her. Annie, the oldest by a year, was so fragile, and Sheridan felt her pain keenly. Sheridan had always been the strong one. She was still the strong one. Still the one looking out for her sister and wishing that she could give Annie some of her strength.

She felt so guilty every time Annie fell apart. It wasn't her fault, and yet she couldn't help but feel responsible. There'd only been enough money in their family for one daughter to go to college, and Sheridan had better grades. Annie had been shy and reclusive while Sheridan was outgoing. The choice had been evident to all of them, but it was yet another thing Sheridan felt guilty over. Maybe if their parents had tried harder to encourage Annie, to support her decisions, she would be stronger than she was. Instead, she let everyone else make her choices.

The one thing she wanted in this life was the one thing she couldn't have. But Sheridan could give it to her. And she was determined to do just that, in spite of this latest wrinkle in the plan.

Eventually, Annie's husband came home and took the phone away. Sheridan talked to Chris for a few minutes and then the line went dead.

She leaned back in her chair and blinked. Her eyes were gritty and swollen from the crying she'd been doing along with her sister. She snatched up a tissue from the holder on her desk and dabbed at her eyes.

How had this all gone wrong? It was supposed to be so easy. Annie couldn't carry a baby to term, but Sheridan could. So she'd offered to have a baby for her sister, knowing that it would make Annie happy and fulfill her deepest desire. It would have also made their parents happy, if they were still alive, to know they'd have a grandchild on the way. They'd had Annie and Sheridan late in life, and they'd desperately wanted grandchildren. But Annie hadn't been able to provide them, and Sheridan hadn't been ready.

Now Sheridan wished she'd had this baby earlier so her parents could have held their grandchild before they died. Though the child wouldn't be Annie's biologically, it would still share her DNA. The Sloane DNA.

Sheridan had gone in for the insemination a week

ago. They still didn't know whether it had worked or not, but now that she knew it wasn't Chris's sperm, she fervently hoped it hadn't.

She'd been given sperm from a different donor. A foreigner. The sperm bank would give them no other information beyond the physical facts. An Arab male, six-two, black hair, dark eyes, healthy.

Sheridan put her hand on her belly and drew in a deep breath. They couldn't test for another week yet. Another week of Annie crying her eyes out. Another week until Sheridan knew if she was having an anonymous man's baby or if they would try again with Chris's sperm.

But what if she was pregnant this time? Then what?

There was a knock on her door, and her partner popped her head in. Sheridan swiped her eyes again and smiled as Kelly came inside the small office at the back of the space they rented for their business.

"Hey, you okay?"

Sheridan sniffed. "Not exactly." She waved a hand. "I will be, but it's just a lot to process."

Kelly came over and took her hand, squeezed it before she sat in a chair nearby and leaned forward to look Sheridan in the eye. "Want to talk about it?"

Sheridan thought she didn't, but then she spilled the news almost as if she couldn't quite help herself. And it felt good to tell someone else. Someone who wouldn't sob and fall apart and need more reassurance than Sheridan knew how to give. If her mother was still alive, she'd know what to say to Annie. But Sheridan so often didn't.

Kelly didn't interrupt, but her eyes grew bigger as the story unfolded. Then she sat back in the chair with her jaw hanging open.

"Wow. So you might be pregnant with another man's baby. Poor Annie! She must be devastated."

Sheridan's heart throbbed. "She is. She'd pinned all her hopes on me having a baby for her and Chris. After so many disappointments, so many treatments and failed attempts of her own, she's fragile right now…." Sheridan sucked in a breath. "This was just a bad time for it to happen."

"I'm so sorry, sweetie. But maybe it won't take, and then you can try again."

"That's what I'm hoping." The doctor had said that sometimes they had to repeat the process two or three times before it was successful. And while it seemed wrong on some level to hope for failure this time, it would also be the best outcome. Sheridan stood and straightened her skirt. "Well, don't we have a party to cater? Mrs. Lands will be expecting her crab puffs and roast beef in a couple of hours."

"It's under control, Sheri. Why don't you just go home and rest? You look like hell, you know."

Sheridan laughed. "Gee, thanks." But then she shook her head. "I'll freshen up, but I'd really like to work. It'll keep my mind occupied."

Kelly looked doubtful. "All right. But if you find yourself crying in the soup, you have to go."

The party was a success. The guests loved the food, the waitstaff did a superb job and once everything was under control, Sheridan went back to the office to work on the menus for the next party they were catering in a few days' time. Kelly stayed behind to make sure there were no last-minute issues, but Sheridan knew her partner would come back to the office after it was over.

They were a great team. Had been since the first moment they'd met in school. Kelly was the cooking talent, and Sheridan was the architect behind the business. Literally the architect, Sheridan thought with a wry smile. She'd gone to the Savannah College of Art and Design for a degree in historical preservation architecture, but it was her talent at organizing parties that helped make Dixie Doin's—they'd left the *g* off *doing* on purpose, which worked well in the South but not so much when visiting Yankees called it *doynes*—into the growing business it was today.

They'd rented a building with a large commercial kitchen, hired a staff and maintained a storefront where people could come in and browse through specialty items that included table linens, dishes, gourmet oils and salts and various teas and teapots.

Sheridan settled in her office to scroll through the requirements for the next event. She had no idea how much time had passed when she heard the buzzer for the shop door. She automatically glanced up at the screen where the camera feed showed different angles of the store. Tiffany, the teenager they'd hired for the summer, was nowhere to be seen. A man stood inside the shop, looking around the room as if he had no clue what he was doing there.

Probably his wife had sent him to buy something and he had no idea what it looked like. Sheridan got up from her desk when Tiffany still hadn't appeared and went out to see if she could help him. Yes, it was annoying, and yes, she would have to speak to the girl again about not leaving the floor, but no way would she let a potential customer walk away when she could do the job herself.

The man was standing with his back to her. He was

tall, black haired and dressed in a business suit. There was something about him that seemed to dwarf the room, but then she shook that thought away. He was just a man. She'd never yet met one who impressed her all that much. Well, maybe Chris, her sister's husband. He loved Annie so much that he would do anything for her.

In Sheridan's experience, most men were far too fickle. And the better looking they were, the worse they seemed to be. On some level, she always fell for it, though. Because she was too trusting of people, and because she liked to believe the best of them. Her mother had always said she was too sunny and sweet. She was working on it, darn it, but what was the point in believing the worst of everyone you met? It was a depressing way to live—even if her last boyfriend had proved that she'd have been better off believing the worst of him from the start.

"Welcome to Dixie Doin's," she said brightly. "Can we help you today, sir?"

The man seemed to stiffen slightly. And then he turned, slowly, until Sheridan found herself holding her breath as she gazed into the most coldly handsome face she'd ever seen. There wasn't an ounce of friendliness in his dark eyes—yet, incongruously, there was an abundance of heat.

Her heart kicked up a level, pounding hard in her chest. She told herself it was the hormones from all the shots and the stress of waiting to see whether or not the fertilization had succeeded.

But it wasn't that. It wasn't even that he was breathtakingly handsome.

It was the fact he was an Arab, when she'd just been told the news of the clinic's mistake. It seemed a cruel joke to be faced with a man like him when she didn't know whether she was pregnant with a stranger's baby or if she could try again for her sister.

"You are Sheridan Sloane."

He said it without even a hint of uncertainty, as if he knew her. But she did not know him—and she didn't like the way he stood there sizing her up as if she was something he might step in on a sidewalk.

She was predisposed to like everyone she met. But this man already rubbed her the wrong way.

"I am." She folded her arms beneath her breasts and tilted her chin up. "And you are?"

She imbued those words with every last ounce of Southern haughtiness she could manage. Sometimes having a family who descended from the *Mayflower* and who boasted a signer of the Declaration of Independence, as well as at least six Patriots who'd fought in the American War of Independence was a good thing. Even if her family had sunk into that sort of gentile poverty that had hit generations of Southerners after Reconstruction, she had her pride and her heritage—and her mother's refined voice telling her that no one had the right to make her feel as if she wasn't good enough for them.

He did something very odd then. He bent slightly at the waist before touching his forehead, lips and heart. Then he stood there so straight and tall and, well, stately, that she got a tingle in her belly. She imagined him in desert robes, doing that very same thing, and gooey warmth flooded her in places that hadn't gotten warm in a very long time.

"I am Rashid bin Zaid al-Hassan."

The door opened again and this time another man entered. He was also in a suit, but he was wearing a headset and she realized with a start that he must be a bodyguard. A quick glance at the street in front of the shop revealed a long, black limousine and another man in a suit. And another stationed on the far side of the street, dark sunglasses covering his eyes as he looked up and down for any signs of trouble.

The one who'd just entered the shop stood by the door without moving. The man before her didn't even seem to notice his presence. Or, more likely, he was so accustomed to it that he ignored it on purpose.

"What can I help you with Mr., er, Rashid." It was the only name she could remember from that string of names he'd spoken.

The man at the door stiffened, but the man before her lifted an eyebrow as if he were somehow amused.

"You have something of mine, Miss Sloane. And I want it back."

A fine sheen of sweat broke out on her upper lip. She hoped like hell he couldn't see it. First of all, it wasn't ladylike. Second, she sensed that any nervousness on her part would be an advantage for him. This was the kind of man who pounced on weakness like a ravenous cat.

"I don't believe we've ever done business with any Rashids, but if we accidentally packed up some of your wife's good silver with our own, you may, of course, have it back."

He no longer looked amused. In fact, he looked downright furious. "You do not have my silver, Miss Sloane."

He took a step toward her then, his large form as graceful and silent as a cat. He was so close she could smell him. He wasn't wearing heavy cologne, but he had a scent like hot summer breezes and crisp spices. Her fanciful imagination conjured up a desert oasis, waving palm trees, a cool spring, an Arabian stallion—and this man, dressed in desert robes like Omar Sharif or Peter O'Toole.

It was a delicious mirage. And disconcerting as hell.

Sheridan put her hand out and smoothed it over the edge of the counter as she tried to appear casual. "If you could just inform me what it is, I'll take a l-look and see if I can find it."

Damn her voice for quavering.

"I doubt you could."

His gaze dropped to her middle, lingered. It took several moments, but then her stomach began a long, slow free fall into nothingness. He couldn't possibly mean—

Oh, no. No, no, no...

But his head lifted and his eyes met hers and she knew he was not here for the family silver.

"How...?" she began. Sheridan swallowed hard. This was unbelievable. An incredible breach of confidentiality. She would sue that clinic into the next millennium. "They wouldn't tell me a thing about you. How did you get them to reveal my information?"

For one wild moment, she hoped he didn't know what she was talking about. That this was indeed some sort of misunderstanding with a tall, beautiful Arab male who meant something entirely different than she thought. He would blink, shake his head, inform her that she had accidentally packed a small family heirloom—though she'd never done such a thing before—when she'd catered his event. Then he would describe it and she would go searching for it as though her life depended on it. Anything to be rid of him and quiet this flame raging inside her as he moved even closer than before.

But she knew, deep down, that he did know what she meant. That there was no misunderstanding.

"I am a powerful man, Miss Sloane. I get what I want. Besides, imagine the scandal were it to become known that an American facility had made such a mistake." His voice dripped of self-righteousness. "Impregnating some random woman with a potential heir to the throne of Kyr? And then refusing to inform the king of the child's whereabouts?"

He shook his head while her insides turned to ice as she tried to process what he'd just said.

"It would not happen," he continued. "It did not happen. As you see."

Sheridan found herself slumping against the counter, her eyes glued to this man's face while the rest of the room began to darken and fade. "D-did you say *king?* They gave me a king's sperm?"

She pressed a shaky hand to her forehead. Her throat was dry, so dry. And her belly wanted to heave. She'd thought this couldn't possibly get worse. She'd been wrong. She swallowed the acidic bitterness and focused on the man before her.

"They did, Miss Sloane."

Oh, my God. Her brain stopped working. She'd thought he was the one whose sperm she'd gotten—he'd said she had something of his, right?—but a king would not come to her shop and tell her these things. A king would also not look so dark and dangerous.

This was someone else. An official. Perhaps even an ambassador. Or an enforcer.

It was easy to believe this man could be hired muscle. He was tall and broad, and his eyes were chips of dark ice. His voice was frosty and utterly compelling. He had come to tell her about this king and to—to…?

She couldn't imagine what he'd come here for. What he expected of her.

Sheridan worked hard to force out the words before the nausea overwhelmed her. "Please tell the king that I'm sorry. I understand how difficult this must be, but he's not the only one affected. My sister—"

She pressed her hand to her mouth as bile rose in her throat. What would she say to Annie? Her fragile sister would implode, she just knew it.

"Sorry is not enough, Miss Sloane. It is not nearly enough."

She swallowed the nausea. Her voice was thready when she spoke. "Then I don't—"

"Are you quite all right?" He was beginning to look alarmed. A much more intriguing look than the angry one he'd been giving her a moment ago.

"I'm fine." Except she didn't feel fine. She felt hot and sweaty and sick to her stomach.

"You look green."

"It's the heat. And the hormones," she added. She pushed away from the counter, her limbs shaking with the effort of holding herself upright. "I should sit down, I think."

She started to take a step, but her knees didn't want to function quite right. Mr. Rashid—or whatever his name was—lashed out and wrapped an arm around her. She found herself wedged tightly against a firm, hard, warm body. Her nerve endings started to crackle and snap with fresh heat.

It was too much, too much, and yet she couldn't get

away. Briefly, a small corner of her brain admitted that she didn't *want* to get away.

He spoke, his voice seeming farther away than before. The words were beautiful, musical, but he did not seem to be speaking them to her. And then he swept her up into his arms as if she weighed nothing and strode across her store on long legs. Her office door opened and he went and sat her down on the small couch she kept for meeting with clients.

She didn't want to let him go, but she did. Her gaze fluttered over to the entry, where saw a wide-eyed Tiffany standing there, and one of the suit-clad men, who reached in and closed the door, leaving Sheridan alone with Mr. Rashid.

He sank down on one knee beside the couch and pressed a hand to her head. She knew what he would find. She was clammy and hot and she uttered a feeble protest. The door opened again and Tiffany appeared with a glass of ice water and a folded cloth.

Sheridan took it and sipped gratefully, letting the coolness wash through her as she closed her eyes and breathed. Someone put the cool cloth on her forehead and she reached up to clutch it because it felt so nice.

She didn't know how long she sat there, holding the cloth and sipping the water, but when she finally opened her eyes and looked up, Mr. Rashid was still there, sitting across from her in one of the pretty Queen Anne chairs she'd bought from a local antiques shop. He looked ridiculous in it, far too big and masculine, but he also looked as if he didn't care.

"What happened?" His voice was not as hard as it had been. She didn't think he was capable of gentleness, and this was as close to it as he got.

"Too much stress, too many hormones, too much summer heat." She shrugged. "Take your pick, Mr. Rashid. It could be any of them."

He muttered something in Arabic and then he was looking at her, his burning gaze penetrating deep. There was frost in his voice. "Miss Sloane, I think you misunderstand something about what's going on here."

Her heart skipped. Why was he so beautiful? And why was he such a contrast? He was fire and ice in one person. Hot eyes, cold heart. It almost made her sad. But why should it? She did not know him, and what she did know so far hadn't endeared him to her. "Do I?"

"Indeed. I am not Mr. Rashid."

"Then who are you?"

He looked haughty and her stomach threatened to heave again. Because there was something familiar about that face, she realized. She'd seen it on the news a few weeks ago.

He spoke, his voice clear and firm and lightly accented. "I am King Rashid bin Zaid al-Hassan, the Great Protector of my people, the Lion of Kyr and Defender of the Throne. And you, Miss Sloane, may be carrying my heir."

CHAPTER TWO

THE WOMAN LOOKED positively frightened. Rashid did not relish making her so, but perhaps it was better if he did. Better if she agreed without question to what she must do. She could not be allowed to stay here in this…this *shop*…and work as if she did not potentially carry the next king of Kyr in her womb.

He had spent the long hours of the flight researching Sheridan Sloane. She was twenty-six, unmarried and part owner of this business that planned and catered various parties in the local area. She had one older sister, a woman named Ann Sloane Campbell, who had been trying to conceive a child for six years now.

Sheridan was supposed to carry the baby her sister could not conceive. It was an admirable enough thing to do, he supposed, but since he'd now been dragged into it, he had his own legacy to protect. If her sister was upset about it, then he could not help that.

Sheridan Sloane was a pretty woman, though not especially striking in any way. She was of average height and small boned, with golden-blond hair of indeterminate length since it was wrapped in a coil on her head. Her eyes, wide as she gazed at him, were a blue so dark they were almost violet. There were bruises under them, marring her pale skin.

She was tired and overwhelmed and no match for him. She was the sort of woman who did what she was told, in spite of her small rebellion earlier. She was a pleaser, and he was not. He would order her to come with him, and she would do it.

But, as he watched her, her body seemed to grow stiff. He could see the shutters closing, the walls rising. It was an unpleasant surprise to find she had a backbone after all. Still, he'd broken stronger people—men, usually—than her.

She shifted until she was sitting fully upright, her feet swinging onto the floor now. She faced him across a small tea table, her eyes snapping with fresh sparks. He was intrigued in spite of himself.

"*You* are the king? You could have said that right away, you know, and saved us a few steps."

He arched an eyebrow. "Yes, but what would you have done then? You nearly fainted when I informed you that you had been inseminated with a king's sperm."

Her lips pursed. "I nearly fainted because it's been a long, stressful day. Do you have any idea how my sister took the news, Mr.—oh, hell, I have no idea what to call you."

"*Your Majesty* will work."

Her face flooded with color. And there went that little chin again, thrusting into the air. Who was she trying to convince that she was a tigress? Him, or herself? Before he could ask, she imbued her voice with steel.

"I realize we find ourselves in an untenable situation, but someone inserted your sperm into my body a few days ago. I think that warrants a first-name basis, don't you? At least until this is resolved."

Rashid would have coughed if he'd been drinking anything. As it was, he could only glare at her. She shocked him. Oddly, she also amused him. It was this last that should alarm him, but in fact it was the first normal thing that had happened to him since he'd taken the throne two months ago.

He shouldn't allow any familiarity between them. But she might be carrying his child—*his child!*—and it seemed wrong to treat her as a complete stranger. He thought of Daria, of her soft brown eyes and swollen belly, and he wanted to stand up and flee this room. But of course he could not do so. He was a king now, and he had a responsibility to his nation. To his people.

And to his child.

Daria would want him to be kind to this woman. So he would try, though it went against his nature to be kind to anyone. He was not cruel; he was indifferent. He'd learned to be so over the hellish years of his childhood. If you did not care, people couldn't hurt you.

When you did… Well, he knew what happened when you cared. He had the scars on his soul to prove it. The only person he cared about these days was Kadir, and that was as much as he was capable of.

He inclined his head briefly. "You may call me Rashid." And then he added, "I suggest, however, you do not do it in front of my staff. They will not understand the informality."

She wrapped her arms around herself and rubbed her upper arms almost absently. "You can call me Sheridan, then. And I don't see why you need worry about your staff. We won't know for another week if there's a baby.

I can call you with the information, if you'd like. Then we can decide what to do if it's necessary."

He blinked at her. She truly did not understand. Or she was being stubbornly obtuse on purpose. His temper rose anew.

"You will not call me."

She frowned at his tone. "Fine. You can call me. Either way, we'll work it out."

He clenched his fingers into fists in his lap. Stubborn woman!

"There is nothing to work out. You have been artificially inseminated with my sperm. You might be carrying the next king of Kyr. There is no possible choice other than the one I offer you now."

"I honestly don't think—"

"Silence, Miss Sloane," he snapped, coming to the end of his tether. "You are not here to think. You will accompany me to the airport, where you will board the royal jet. We will be in Kyr by morning, and you will be shown every courtesy while we await the results. Should you fail to conceive my child, you will be escorted home again."

Her jaw had dropped as he talked. He tried not to focus on the pink curve of her lower lip. It glistened with moisture and he found himself wanting to lean forward and touch his tongue just there to see if she tasted as sweet and delicate as she looked.

The thought shocked him. And angered him. He did not want this woman.

She was shaking her head almost violently now. A lock of hair dropped from her twist and curved in front of her cheekbone. She impatiently tucked it behind an ear.

"I can't drop everything and go away with you! I have a business to run. And my bank account, unlike yours, I'm sure, isn't bursting with money. No way. No way in hell."

Her response stunned him. He shot to his feet then, his temper beginning to boil. He had a country to run and one crisis after another to solve these days. He had a council waiting for him, a stack of dossiers on potential brides to scour through and an upcoming meeting with kings from surrounding nations to discuss oil production, mineral rights and reciprocity agreements.

And yet he was being thwarted by one small, irritating woman who refused to give an inch of ground in this battle. A people pleaser? She didn't look as if she cared one bit about pleasing him at the moment.

Rashid gave her the look that made the palace staff tremble. "I wasn't giving you a choice, Miss Sloane."

She sucked in a breath, and he knew he had her.

But then her face reddened and her eyes flashed purple fire and Rashid stood there in shock.

"You think you have the right to make decisions for me? This is America and I don't have to go anywhere with you. Not only that, but I *won't* go. If I'm pregnant, we'll figure it out. But as of this moment, we do not know that. I can't just leave because you wish it. Nor do I intend to."

His entire body vibrated with fury. He was not accustomed to being told no. Not by his employees at Hassan Oil—a company he'd built on his own and still owned to this day, even if he'd had to turn over the day-to-day operations to a CEO—not by his staff in the palace, not by anyone anywhere in the past several years. He was an al-Hassan, with money and influence, and people did not tell him no.

And now he was a king, and they *really* did not tell him no.

But Sheridan Sloane had. She sat there on her couch, looking pale and delicate and too small to safely carry a baby for nine months, and spoke to him like he was her gardener. It infuriated him. And stunned him, too, if he was willing to admit it.

No matter how much he admired her fighting spirit, he would not be merciful. He'd left mercy behind a long time ago.

"Miss Sloane," he said, very coolly and clearly. "It would be unwise to anger me. This business you run?" He snapped his fingers. "I could destroy it in a moment. I could destroy *you* in a moment. Continue to defy me, and I shall."

Sheridan's pulse skipped and slid like it was tumbling down a hill and couldn't find purchase. He'd just threatened her. Threatened Dixie Doin's. At first she wanted to laugh him off. But then she looked at him standing there, at his tall, dark form and the dark glitter of his eyes, and knew he was not only perfectly serious, but that he was also probably capable of accomplishing it.

He was a king. *A king!*

Of an incredibly rich, oil-producing nation in the Arabian Desert. She knew where Kyr was. Hadn't they just had a crisis that was plastered all over the news? The king had been very ill and no one had known who his successor was going to be.

She'd found it fascinating that a monarch could choose his successor from among his sons, and puzzling that he had not done so by that point. They were grown after all, and he must surely know which of them was best suited to the job.

The fact he had not done so surely spoke volumes about him—or about his children. She wasn't sure which.

But the crisis had passed and Kyr had a king. This man. Rashid bin Zaid al-Hassan. Oh, yes, his name was imprinted on her memory now. She would never forget it again as long as she lived.

Still, she had not been raised to blindly follow orders and she would not start now. Even though he terrified her on some level. He was so cold and angry, and he was a king. But he was not *her* king. Hadn't her ancestors fought to divest themselves of kings?

Sheridan cleared her throat. "It's only seven more days until the test. You could stay in Savannah. Or maybe you could come back when the results are due. It seems far simpler than what you're proposing."

He did not look in the least bit appeased. "Does it, now? Because your business, which has another owner and employees to help, needs your presence far more than a nation needs her king, yes? How extraordinary, Miss Sloane."

Sheridan pushed the stray lock of hair behind her ear again. How did he manage to make her feel petty when all she wanted was to continue to live her life as normally as possible until the moment when she found out if everything was going to change or not? She didn't even want to contemplate what it would mean if she *were* carrying this man's child.

A royal baby. Madness.

She twisted the cloth that she'd earlier pressed to her

forehead. "I didn't mean to suggest any such thing. But yes, my business is important to me, and I can't leave Kelly to do everything by herself. I have menus to plan, and supplies to buy—"

"And I have a peace agreement to broker and a nation to run." He'd already dismissed her, she realized. He slipped a phone from his pocket and put it to his ear. And then he was speaking in mellifluous Arabic to someone on the other end. When he finished, cool dark eyes raked over her again. "You will come, Miss Sloane, and you will do it now. My lawyer has instructions to purchase your loan from the bank. I assure you he will accomplish this, as I am willing to offer far more than this business is worth."

Sheridan's jaw dropped even as a fine sheen of sweat broke out between her breasts. He was quite easily the most obnoxious man she'd ever met. And the most attractive.

No. The most evil man. Yes, definitely that. Evil.

Because she knew he was not bluffing. A man who had the power to obtain her information from the fertility clinic—information protected by law—as if it was freely available to anyone who asked, was not a man to make bluffs.

He had the power to buy Dixie Doin's and do whatever he wanted with it. Close the doors. Put people out of work. Ruin hers and Kelly's dream. She didn't care so much for herself right now, but Kelly? Kelly had been so kind when Sheridan told her she wanted to have a baby for Chris and Annie, even though it would impact the business for her to be pregnant.

Not to mention the impact while Sheridan went through the insemination process. You just didn't show up at the clinic one day and ask for sperm after all, and Kelly had stoically accepted it all without even a hint of disapproval or fear.

So how could she allow this overbearing, rude tyrant of a man to ruin Kelly's dream just because Sheridan wanted so very desperately to defy him?

She couldn't.

She rose on shaky feet and faced him. He was so very tall, so overwhelming, but she faced him head on with her chin up and her back straight. She pulled in a breath that shook with anger.

"Am I to be allowed to collect any clothing? Surely I need my passport."

She thought he would look satisfied or triumphant at her capitulation, but he in fact looked bored. As if he'd never doubted she would agree. She hated him in that moment, and Sheridan had never hated anyone in her life.

"You do not need a passport if you are traveling with me. But we will make a brief stop at your home. You will get what you need for the next week."

Fear skirted the edges of her anger. Was she truly proposing to board a plane to a far-off nation where she didn't speak the language and didn't understand the customs? But how could she refuse? If she did, he would ruin Dixie Doin's and put them out of business. All the money she and Kelly had invested would be gone.

But what happened in a week? Would he force her to stay in Kyr forever if she were carrying his child?

Sheridan put a hand to her mouth to press back the sudden cry welling up in her throat. In reality, she was being kidnapped by a desert king, forced into a harem for all she knew, and there was nothing she could do about it.

Not if she wanted to protect her friend and her employees. Not to mention Annie and Chris. What would this man do to them if she didn't comply? Could he get Chris fired? He could certainly buy the loan on their house—they'd mortgaged it to the hilt to pay for one failed fertility treatment after another—and then what?

Ice formed in her veins. He would throw them out of their home with no sympathy or shame. She could see it in his eyes, in the hard set to his jaw. This man was ruthless and incapable of empathy.

"How do I know I'll be safe?" Sheridan asked, her voice smaller than she would have liked.

His brows drew down swiftly as his anger flared. "Safe? Do you think me a barbarian, Miss Sloane? A terrorist? I am a king and you are my honored guest. You will have every luxury for the duration of your stay in Kyr."

She swallowed at the vehemence in his tone. "And what if I'm pregnant? What then?"

Because she had to know. For herself, for the child. She had to know what this man would do, what he would expect.

His icy gaze sharpened in a way that sent a shiver rippling through her. "You were planning to give the child away. Why would this change?"

An unexpected arrow of pain dived into her belly, hollowing out a space there. Yes, she'd been planning to give the baby up. But to her sister. Carrying a child for Annie and Chris was one thing. She would not be the baby's mother, even if she was the biological mother, but she would still be part of his or her life. An aunt who would spoil the child of her body rotten, kiss and hug him, buy him presents, shower him with love.

But to give her baby to a stranger, even if the stranger was the other half of the child's DNA?

It went against everything she felt inside.

"I won't give up my baby." Her voice was hoarse. But what choice did she have? He would destroy everyone she loved.

His eyes glittered like ice and she trembled inside. "Yes, I see," he murmured after a long moment. "I am a king, and my son will be a king. Why would you willingly relinquish a child so valuable?"

Sheridan had never wanted to harm another human being in her life, but if she could slap this one and get away with it, she would. He was evil, hateful. Her face flooded with heat and her stomach flipped, but this time it wasn't a sickening flip so much as an angry one.

"You're disgusting," she spat. "I don't care how amazing and fabulous you think you are, but until today I'd never heard of you." *A small lie.* "My feelings about this baby have nothing to do with who you are and everything to do with the fact he *or* she is half mine."

She lifted a shaking finger and pointed at the door. He didn't own her, and until they knew whether or not she was pregnant, she wasn't going anywhere with him. It was a risk, but she needed time to figure out what to do, time to consult an attorney and talk to her family. If she left the country with him, it was over. He would own her and any baby within her.

"You should leave."

He stared at her for a long moment, that handsome

countenance wreathed in dark anger. And then he burst out laughing. It shocked her. The sound was so rich, so beautiful. And chilling in a way.

"I don't see what's so funny," she said, her heart fluttering like a hummingbird's wings. "I am perfectly serious. I'll see you in court, *Your Majesty*."

The door opened behind her. She turned, hoping it was Kelly or even Tiffany coming to save her, but it was merely one of the bodyguards.

"The car is ready, Your Majesty."

"Excellent."

Sheridan turned toward the king, but he'd moved when she'd been looking at his bodyguard. Before she knew what he was about, he swept an arm behind her knees and jerked her into his arms. Once more, she was pressed against his hard, taut body, his scent in her nostrils, conjuring images of heat and sand and cool water. A hot, tight feeling flared beneath her skin, burning through her and stopping the breath in her chest until he was halfway across the storefront.

There were customers, she noted vaguely. And Tiffany, who looked up as Rashid al-Hassan walked by with Sheridan in his arms. Tiffany didn't even look surprised, the silly girl. She just looked bored, like always.

Sheridan knew she needed to scream. She needed to get these people's attention and get this man to put her down immediately. She felt her lungs working again—of course they'd never stopped, but she hadn't felt them, hadn't felt anything but heat and unbearable want when he'd picked her up—and she sucked in air, preparing to release it in the most eardrum-shattering cry she could manage.

But she never got the chance because Rashid al-

Hassan—the Great Protector of his people, the Lion of Kyr and Defender of the Throne—dropped his mouth over hers and silenced her.

CHAPTER THREE

RASHID HADN'T MEANT to kiss her. But the damned woman was going to scream and he could not allow it. So he'd silenced her in the only way he could.

Her mouth was soft and pliant and sweet. He took advantage of the fact her lips were open to slip his tongue inside and stroke across the velvety softness of her mouth. She didn't move for a long moment and he began to wonder if she would bite him.

She was certainly capable of it. He'd not encountered a woman such as this one in…well, ever. Usually, women softened around him. Their eyes got big and wide and their mouths fell open invitingly. They sighed. They purred. They pouted.

They did not act as if he were poison. They did not glare daggers at him and spit fire and tell him to get out in prim little voices that belonged to the starchy librarians he'd encountered when he'd gone to university.

Sheridan's breath hitched in and he knew he had her. Knew she was his, for the moment.

He deepened the kiss, demanding more of a response from her. He had to keep her mouth busy and her thoughts focused on him until he could get her out of the store and into the car. It was a mercenary act on his part and he had no trouble pushing it as far as he needed in order to keep the fool woman silenced.

Her mouth opened a little wider, her tongue stroking tentatively against his.

Rashid's body turned to stone in a heartbeat. He had not expected that. But then he reminded himself there was a reason for his reaction. It had been a while since he'd had a woman. Being king had taken all his time these past couple of months. He was no longer a private citizen. No longer a man who could walk into a club, spot a gorgeous woman and take her home for a night of hot sex and no recriminations.

He was a king, and kings did not go anywhere without an entourage. They also did not pick up women and take them back to the palace for sex.

Certainly, he could have sent for a woman. But what kind of man would he be if he sent others to pick out women for him for the express purpose of having sex?

He was no prude, and he figured what people did with their bodies was their own business, but he'd never paid for sex in his life and he wasn't going to start now. Because that was what it would be if he ordered a woman for the evening as if she were an item on a room service menu.

Oh, she would not be a common prostitute. She wouldn't be a prostitute at all. But that didn't make it any better in his mind.

Another reason why he was going to have to choose a wife soon from the handful of princesses and heiresses his council had recommended. And yet he couldn't imagine having sex with any of the women whose dossiers he'd been sent thus far, much less facing one of them across a breakfast table for the rest of his life.

Damn Kadir for forcing him to take the throne. Yes, Rashid had always wanted to be king, but he hadn't quite realized how very confined he would feel. He was a ruler, a man with the power of life and death over his subjects, a man with absolute authority—and he had no private life to speak of. No one with whom he could share the simple pleasures.

He had not thought that would bother him so much, but it did. He missed Daria. Missed having someone in his life who loved him because of his flaws, not in spite of them. But Daria was gone, and there was no one.

Sheridan shifted in his arms and he felt her confusion, her hesitation. She was fighting herself, fighting her nature, and if he'd learned anything about her in these last few minutes, he knew she would conquer her baser instincts and fight against him soon enough.

A people pleaser? Perhaps she was, but she was not a Rashid pleaser. He knew that well enough now.

Because he was angry, because he was frustrated, he took the kiss to another level, ravaged her mouth like a man starved. He wanted to confuse her, wanted to keep her quiet and, hell, yes, he wanted to disconcert her. How dare she disobey him?

She gripped his lapels, twisted her fists in them. And then she met him as savagely as he met her. His body responded with a surge of heat he'd not felt in a long time. Her breath grew shallower and she made a sound in her throat.

He broke the kiss then, uncertain if he was pushing her too far too fast. Alarmed at his body's reaction to her, he tucked her head against his chest before she could speak.

"Quiet, *habibti*. Let me get you home." He smiled

at the women in the shop who threw them astonished looks and then strode outside and down the front steps before Sheridan could regain her ability to think clearly.

The car door swung smoothly open and Rashid bent to place Sheridan on the seat. She was so small and light that it was like handling a piece of china. He didn't want to break her, but he also knew she was stronger than she looked.

He got in beside her, the door sealed shut, and the car slid smoothly away from the curb and down the sun-dappled streets. The partition was up between them and the driver, and silence hung heavy in the car.

"You kidnapped me." Her voice was small and frightened and Rashid swung to look at her. Her golden hair gleamed in the sunlight that filtered into the car and her eyes were wide with fear. He did not enjoy that, but he told himself it was necessary. Whatever it took to force her to obey.

Rashid sat back and tugged a sleeve into place. He was not precisely pleased with himself, and yet he'd done what had to be done. A man like him claimed his child. And the woman carrying it.

"I did warn you."

"You said you weren't a barbarian." Her hands clenched into fists in her lap. She wore a pink dress and smelled like cotton candy and Rashid wanted to lean into her and press his nose to her hair.

"Indeed."

"Then I must be confused, because I thought barbarians did precisely what you just did. Or did you perhaps say you weren't a *barber* and I simply misunderstood?"

And there was the attitude. Clearly, she was not

damaged in any way. It gave his temper permission to emerge.

"I am a desert king. Of course I'm a barbarian. Isn't that what you believe? Because I speak Arabic and come from a nation where the men wear robes and the women are veiled, that I must surely be less civilized than you?"

Her lips pressed into a tight, white line. "Even if I didn't believe it, don't you think you just proved it? What kind of man kidnaps a woman he's never met just because there's been a mix-up in the clinic?"

Her eyes were flashing purple fire again. For some reason, that intrigued him almost as much as it angered him.

"A man who has no time for arguments. A man who holds the lives of an entire nation in his hands and who needs to get back to his duties. A man who has no reason whatsoever to trust that the woman carrying his heir will turn over the child when it is time."

Her eyes darkened with anger. "I won't give up my baby just because you wish it."

"You were willing to do so for your sister."

"That's different and you know it. I would still be part of the child's life. A beloved aunt." She shook her head suddenly. "Why are we arguing about this? There's no guarantee I'm pregnant. It doesn't always work the first time."

"Perhaps not, but I will take no chances. My child will be a king one day, Sheridan Sloane. He will not be raised in an apartment in America by a woman who works sixteen-hour days and ignores him in favor of her own interests."

Her skin flushed bright red. "How dare you?" she growled. "How dare you act as if you know me when you don't have the faintest clue? I would never ignore my child. Never!"

He infuriated her. No, she'd not planned for a child in her life—the baby was supposed to be Annie's—but the fact he would sit there and smugly inform her that he believed she would neglect her baby in favor of her business made her defensive and angry. Of course she would still have to work, but she would figure it out.

Except there would be no figuring it out. This man was a king, and if she was pregnant, he wasn't going to abandon her to raise the child alone. He would be a part of her life from now on.

Sheridan shivered at the thought. How did one work out custody with a king?

"This baby is supposed to be Annie's," she said, working hard to keep the panic from her voice. "I hadn't planned on a baby of my own, but that doesn't mean I would be a bad or neglectful mother. And I won't let you steamroll right over me just because you're a king. I have rights, too."

His eyes were hooded as he studied her. Did he have to be so damned beautiful? She'd never seen hair so black or eyes so fathomless. If he was an actor, she'd wonder if his cheekbones were the work of a plastic surgeon. His face was a study in perfection, angles and planes and smooth, bronzed skin. He was golden, as if he spent long hours under the sun, and there were fine lines at the corners of his eyes where they crinkled as he studied her.

Her gaze focused on his mouth, those firm, beautiful lips that had pressed against hers. She felt a fresh wave of heat creeping up her throat. He'd only kissed her to shut her up, but she'd forgotten for long minutes why that was a bad thing. His mouth had ravaged hers and she'd only wanted more. Even now, her lips tingled with the memory of his assault on them. She was bruised and swollen, but in a good way. In the kind of way that said a woman had been well kissed and had enjoyed every moment of it.

Sheridan dropped her gaze from his, suddenly self-conscious. It had been a long time since she'd kissed anyone. A long time since she'd lain in bed with a man and felt the heat and wonder of joining her body with another. She hadn't thought she was deprived. Rather, she'd thought she was busy and that she just didn't have time to invest in a relationship.

But now that he'd kissed her, she felt as if she'd been starving for affection. As if the drought in her sex life was suddenly much larger than she'd thought it was. How could he make her feel this way when he was not a nice man?

After her last relationship, a short-lived romance with a womanizing accountant who'd made her feel like the only woman in his life until the moment she'd caught him with his tongue down someone else's throat, she'd vowed to only date nice, trustworthy men.

Rashid al-Hassan was definitely not a nice man. Or trustworthy. But he made things hum and spark inside her, damn him. She'd only kissed him once, but already she wanted to lean forward, tunnel her fingers through that thick mane of hair and claim his lips for another round.

Insanity, Sheridan.

"Surely there is something you want more than this child," he said smoothly, cutting into her thoughts, and her heart began to beat a crazy rhythm.

"No."

He lifted an eyebrow in that superior arch she despised. "Money? I can give you quite a lot of it, you know. Once our divorce is final, you could be a wealthy woman."

Divorce? Her stomach fell to the floor at the thought of being married to this man for even an hour.

"I don't want your money. And I'm definitely not going to marry you." There was only one thing she wanted. It also wasn't something he could give. Unless he had the power of miracles.

She was certain he did not. If a dozen doctors couldn't fix Annie's fertility issues, then neither could a king, no matter how arrogant and entitled.

"Everyone has a price, Sheridan. And if you are pregnant, you most certainly *will* be my wife. In name only, of course. My child will not be born illegitimate."

Her name on his lips was too exotic, too sensual. It stroked over her senses, set up a drumbeat in her veins. And embarrassed her because he clearly wasn't suffering from an unwanted attraction, too. *In name only.*

"All I want is a baby for my sister. And I intend to give her one."

"After you give me my heir, of course."

Her lips tightened. "You make it sound so cold and clinical. As if you're selecting a prized broodmare to give you a champion foal."

The car glided through the streets. Outside the windows, people behaved as usual. Tourists chattered excitedly and pointed from their seats in the horse-drawn carriages that traveled through Savannah's historic district. Part of Sheridan wanted to open the door and run when the car came to a standstill in traffic.

But there was no escape. Not like this anyway. The only way to fight a man like him was with lawyers, and even that was no guarantee because he could afford far better representation than she could.

"It is a clinical thing, is it not?" His voice was rich and smooth and crusted in ice. "We have never been intimate, and yet you may be pregnant with my child. Put there with a syringe in a doctor's office. How is this not clinical?"

Sheridan swallowed the lump in her throat. "I was supposed to be having a baby for my sister. With my brother-in-law's sperm. What would you propose we do differently?"

Of course, it would have been cheaper and easier for her and Chris to just sleep together until she was pregnant, but what a horrifying thought that was. He was her sister's husband and her friend, and there was no way in hell. Lying on a table with her feet in stirrups might be clinical, but it was the only solution.

He ignored the question. "Nevertheless, it is my sperm you received. How do you think this makes me feel?"

She swung around to look at him. Up to this point, she hadn't thought of how it must have affected him. She was almost ashamed of herself for the lapse. Almost.

That ended when she met his gaze. He was looking at her as coldly as ever. King Rashid al-Hassan was a block of ice. A block of ice that had burned strangely hot when he'd pressed his mouth to hers.

Sheridan nervously smoothed the fabric of her dress. "I admit I hadn't thought of it. I imagine you're angry."

"That is one way of putting it." His dark eyes flashed. "I am a king and my country has laws I must obey. You may think us barbarians, but there is a certain logic to the king depositing sperm in a bank outside his nation. It was never meant to be used. Or not under normal circumstances."

She didn't want to think about what kind of circumstances would precipitate using the sperm, but she imagined it would involve his untimely death and no heir to follow him to the throne. She might not like him, but she wouldn't wish him dead.

Yet.

"No, I can see how it might be useful. It's forward thinking to do such a thing."

"Apparently not, when mistakes such as this are allowed to occur."

Sheridan put her hand over her middle instinctively. Fresh anger swirled in her belly. "Calling this baby a mistake is unlikely to inspire my confidence, don't you think? You want me to give him or her up, but you speak as if you don't care about him other than as your heir."

"He will be my heir. Until there is another child, at least."

Her heart thumped. "Because you can choose your successor in Kyr. Of course." Her fingers tightened over her flat belly. She didn't even know if there was a baby in there yet, but already she felt protective and angry.

"It is the way of our people."

Maybe so, but it seemed a horrible way for children to grow up. Talk about an unhealthy sense of competition. "You weren't chosen until right before your father died. How did that make you feel?"

His eyes glittered hot and she had the feeling she'd tweaked the lion's tail. He looked at her as if he would snap her in two with one fierce bite. Yet his voice was still as icy as ever.

"You push me too far, Sheridan Sloane. You should be more cautious."

Maybe she should, but she couldn't seem to do so. "Why? Because you might kidnap me or something?"

His dark eyes raked over her. "Or something."

CHAPTER FOUR

KYR WAS HOT. Savannah was hot, too, but it was also muggy because they were so near the ocean. Kyr was not muggy, though the Persian Gulf was nearby. It was just hot, with the kind of heat that sucked all the moisture right out of you and left you gasping for breath. It was also beautiful, which Sheridan had not expected.

The desert sands were almost red and the dunes rose high in the distance, undulating like waves on the ocean. As they'd approached the city from the airport, she'd viewed tall date palms that grew in ordered rows. Sheridan had been in the same car with Rashid, but once they'd arrived at the palace she'd been taken to what appeared to be a lonely wing with no one else in it. If he had a harem, this was not it.

She still couldn't believe she was here. She paced around the cavernous room of the suite she'd been shown to and marveled at the architecture. There were soaring arches, mosaics of delicate and colorful tile and painted walls and ceilings. There was a sunken area in the middle of the room, lined with colorful cushions, and above her the ceiling soared into a dome shape that was punctuated with small windows, which let light filter down to the floor and spread in warm puddles across its gleaming tiles.

It was a beautiful and lonely space. Sheridan sank onto the cushions and sat by herself in that big room, listening to nothing. There was no television, no radio, no telephone that she could find. She had her cell phone, but no signal.

She leaned back against the cushions and swore she wouldn't cry. For someone like her, a person who craved light and sound and activity, this silent cavern was torture. Just yesterday—had it really been only yesterday?—she'd been surrounded by people at Mrs. Lands's party. And then she'd been in her office, with her beautiful store outside her door, listening to the sounds of people on the street and the low hum of her radio as it played the latest top-forty hits.

She hadn't exactly been happy, not after the news from the clinic and Annie's reaction, but she'd been far more content than she'd given herself credit for. Tears pushed against her eyes at the thought of all she'd left behind, but she didn't let them fall.

Rashid al-Hassan was a tyrant. He'd swept into her life, swept her up against her will and deposited her here alone. And all because the stupid sperm bank had used the wrong sperm. She'd wanted to give her sister a precious gift, but she was here, a veritable prisoner to a rude, arrogant, sinfully attractive man who had all the warmth and friendliness of an iceberg.

He hadn't let her call anyone until they were on his plane. She was still astounded at the opulence of the royal jet. It was one of the most amazing things she'd ever seen, with leather and gold and fine carpets. The bath had even been made of marble. Marble on a jet!

It had also been bigger than her bathroom in her apartment. There were uniformed flight attendants who performed their duties with bright smiles and soft words—and deep bows to their king. She could hardly forget that sight. Any time anyone on that plane had come close to Rashid al-Hassan, they'd dipped almost to the floor. He hadn't even deigned to notice half the time.

It stunned her and unnerved her. She kept telling herself he was just a man, but there hadn't been a single person on that plane who'd acted like he was. When she'd finally been allowed to phone Kelly and Chris—not Annie, goodness, no—she'd held the phone tightly in her hand and explained as best she could that she would be gone for the next week.

They'd taken the news of Rashid much better than she had. Kelly, always a hopeless romantic, had wanted to know if he was handsome and if she would have to marry him. Sheridan had clutched the phone tight and hadn't told her friend that even though Rashid expected her to marry him, she'd rather marry a shark. She'd just said they were taking this one day at a time and would deal with a pregnancy when and if it happened. As if Rashid was reasonable and kind instead of an unfeeling block of stone.

Chris had told her to be strong, and not to worry about Annie. It would all be fine, he'd said. She'd had to bite her lip to keep from crying at the thought of Chris telling her sister the news, but she'd thanked him and told him she'd be in touch.

She spread her fingers over her abdomen. What would become of her if there were a baby inside here?

She stared up at the beam of sunlight filtering into her prison and pressed her fist to her mouth to contain her sob. Nine months as his wife in name only, his prisoner, shut away from the world—and then he would coldly divorce her and send her on her way with empty arms.

Despair filled her until she thought she would choke with it. Soon there was a noise at the entrance to her prison. A woman in a dress and wearing a scarf over her head came in and sat a tray down on a table nearby. Sheridan shot to her feet and went over to where the woman was removing covers from dishes.

"That smells lovely." She was surprised when her stomach growled, especially considering how queasy she'd been feeling since Rashid had come to the store yesterday.

The woman gave her a polite smile. "His Majesty says you must eat, miss."

Must. Of course he did. And as much as she would love to defy him, she wasn't so stupid as to starve herself just to prove a point.

"Can you please tell me where His Majesty is? I would like to speak with him."

Because she was going to go quietly insane if she had to remain in this room alone with no stimulation. The books—and there were plenty of them—were written in Arabic.

The woman shook her head and kept smiling. "Eat, miss."

She gave Sheridan a half bow and glided gracefully toward the door. Sheridan thought about it for two seconds and then followed her. But the woman was through the door and the door shut before Sheridan could reach it.

She jerked it open only to be confronted with the same thing she'd been confronted with earlier: a man in desert robes standing in the corridor, arms crossed, sword strapped to his side. He looked at her no less coolly than his boss had.

"I want to speak to King Rashid," she said.

The man didn't move or speak.

Anger welled up inside her, pressing hard against the confines of her skin until she thought she might burst with it. She started toward the guard. He was big and broad, but she was determined that she would walk past him and keep going until she found people.

The man stepped into her path and she had to stop abruptly or collide nose first with his chest.

"Get out of my way." She glared up at him, but he didn't seem in the least bit concerned. She gathered her courage and ducked the other way. But he was there, in front of her, his big body blocking her progress.

Fury howled deep in her gut. She was in a strange place, being guarded by a huge man who wouldn't speak to her, and she was lonely and furious and scared all at once.

So she did something she had never done in her life. She stomped on his foot.

And gasped. Whatever he was wearing, it was a lot harder than her delicate little sandal. She resisted the urge to clutch her foot and hop around in circles. Barely. The mountain of a man didn't even make a noise. He just took her firmly by the arm and steered her back into the suite. And then he shut the door on her so that she stood there staring at the carved wood with her jaw hanging open. Her foot and her pride stung. She thought about yanking open the door and trying again, like an annoying fly, but she knew she'd only get more of the same from him.

She stood with her hands on her hips, her gaze moving around the room, her brain churning. And then she halted on the tray of food. The tray was big, solid, possibly made of silver. It would be heavy.

Sheridan closed her eyes and pulled in a deep breath. She wasn't really thinking of sneaking into the hall and braining the poor guard, was she? That wasn't nice. He was only doing what he'd been ordered to do. It wasn't polite to smack him with the tray when she really wanted to smack Rashid al-Hassan instead.

She opened her eyes again, continued her circuit of the room. There were windows. All that glass would make a hell of a noise if she busted it. Part of her protested that it was an extreme idea, that a lady didn't go around breaking other people's property. Worse, an architect who specialized in historical preservation didn't go around breaking windows in old palaces, even if the glass was a modern addition to the structure. Which she could tell by the tint and finish.

But this could hardly be termed a normal circumstance. King Rashid al-Hassan had already made the first move, and it hadn't been polite or considerate. So why should she be polite in return?

Game on....

Rashid had just settled in for lunch after a long morning spent in meetings with his council when Mostafa hurried into his office, a wide-eyed look on his face. The man dropped into a deep bow before rising again.

"Speak," Rashid said, knowing Mostafa would not do so until told.

"Majesty, it's the woman."

Rashid went still, his hand hovering over a dish of rice and chicken. He set the spoon down. *The woman* was such an inadequate description for Sheridan Sloane, but if he tried to point that out to Mostafa, the man would think him cracked in the head.

"What about her, Mostafa?"

"She has, er, broken a window. And she is asking to see you."

A prickle of alarm slid through him. "Is she hurt?"

"A few small cuts."

Rashid was on his feet in a second. Steely anger hardened in his veins as he strode out the door and down the corridors of the palace toward the women's quarters. He'd placed her there because it was supposed to be safe—and also because he didn't quite know what to do with her now that he had her here. He'd sent his father's remaining two wives to homes of their own, ostensibly in preparation for taking his own wife—or wives—but in truth he'd wanted to rid the palace of their presence.

They were women his father had married later in life, and so they were much younger than King Zaid had been. Rashid had no idea what kind of relationship his father had had with either of them, but they made him think too often of his father's tempestuous relationship with his own mother. Rashid would not live with women who reminded him of those dark days.

Palace workers dropped to their knees as he passed, a giant wave of obeisance that he hardly noticed. He kept going until he reached the women's suite and the mountainous form of Daoud, the guard he'd placed here.

Daoud fell to his knees and pressed his forehead to the floor. "Forgive me, Your Majesty."

"What happened?"

Daoud looked up from the floor and Rashid made an impatient motion. The man had been with him for years now, long before Rashid became king. Daoud stood. "The woman tried to leave. I prevented her."

"Did you harm her?" His voice was a whip and Daoud paled.

"No, Your Majesty. I took her by the arm, placed her inside the room and closed the door. A few minutes later, I heard the crash."

Rashid brushed past him and went into the room. One tall window was open to the outside. Hot air and fine grains of sand rushed inside along with the sounds of activity on the palace grounds below. Two men worked to clean up the glass that had blown across the floor.

Sheridan sat on cushions in the middle of the room, looking small and dejected. There were a couple of small red lines on her arms and his heart clenched tight. But the ice he lived with on a daily basis didn't fail him. It rushed in, filled all the dark corners of his soul and hardened any sympathetic feelings he may have had for her.

Sheridan looked up then. "And the mighty king has come to call."

"Out," Rashid said to the room in general. The servants who were busy picking up the glass rose and hurried out the door. A woman appeared from the direction of the bath. She dropped a small bowl and cloth on the side table and then she left, as well.

The door behind him sealed shut. Rashid stalked toward the small woman on the cushions. Her golden-blond hair was down today. It hit him with a jolt that it was long and silky and perfectly straight. She was wearing flat white sandals with little jewels set on the bands and a light blue dress with tiny flowers on it. She did not look like a woman who might be carrying a royal baby.

She looked like a misbehaving girl, fresh and pretty and filled with mischief.

And sporting small cuts to her flesh. Cuts she'd caused, he reminded himself. She picked up the cloth and dabbed at her hand. The white fabric came away pink.

"What did you do, Miss Sloane?"

As if he couldn't tell. The window was open to the heat and a silver tray lay discarded to one side. Such violence in such a small package. It astonished him.

She wouldn't look at him. "I admit it was childish of me, but I was angry." Then her violet eyes lifted to his. "I don't ordinarily act this way, I assure you. But you put me here with nothing to do and no one to talk to."

"And this is how you behave when you don't get your way?"

Her gaze didn't waver. In fact, he thought it flickered with anger. Or maybe it was fear. That gave him pause. She had no reason to fear him. Daria would be ashamed of him for scaring this woman.

He tried to look unperturbed. He didn't think it was working based on the way her throat moved as he stared back at her.

"In fact, I realize that we can't always have our way," she said primly. "But this is my first time as a prisoner, and I thought perhaps the rules were different. So I decided to do something about it."

Rashid blinked. "Prisoner?" He spread his hands to encompass the room. It was plush and comfortable and feminine. He remembered it from when he was a child, but he'd not entered these quarters in many years. They hadn't changed much, he decided. "I've been in exclusive hotels that lacked accommodations this fine. You think this is a prison?"

A small shard of guilt pricked him even as he spoke. His rooms with Kadir had been opulent, too, and he'd always thought of them as a cage from which he couldn't wait to escape. Beautiful surroundings did not make a person happy. He knew that better than most.

And she looked decidedly unhappy. "Even the cheapest hotels tend to have televisions. And computers, radios, telephones. There are plenty of books here, I'll grant you that—but I can't read them because they aren't in English."

Rashid's brows drew down. He turned and looked around the room. And realized that she was correct. There was no television, no computer, nothing but furniture and fabric and walls. When the women left, they'd taken their belongings with them. Clearly, they'd considered the electronics to be theirs, too.

"I will have that corrected."

"Which part, Rashid?"

He nearly startled at the sound of his name on her lips. He hadn't forgotten that he'd told her she could call him by name, but he somehow hadn't expected it here and now. Her voice was soft, her accent buttery and sweet.

He suddenly wanted her to speak again, to say his name so he could marvel at how it sounded when she did. Deliciously foreign. Soft.

He shoved away such ridiculous thoughts. "I will have a television installed. And a computer. Whatever you need for your comfort."

"But I am still a prisoner."

He clenched his jaw. "You are not a prisoner. You are my guest. Your every comfort is assured."

"And what if I want to talk to people? Have things to do besides watch television all day? I'm a businesswoman, Rashid. I don't sit around my home and do nothing all day."

"I will find a companion for you."

She sighed heavily. And then she went back to dabbing the cuts on the back of her hand. His anger flared hot again.

"You could have hurt yourself far worse than you did," he growled. "Did you even consider the baby when you behaved so foolishly?"

Her head snapped up, guilt flashing in her gaze. "I've already admitted it was a mistake. And yes, I considered what I was doing before I acted. But I didn't expect the glass to shatter everywhere like that. I threw the tray from a distance, but I guess I threw it harder than I thought."

She'd thrown the tray. At the window. She could have been seriously hurt, the foolish woman. But she sat there looking contrite and dejected—and yes, defiant, too—and he wanted to shake her. And tell her he was sorry.

Now where had that come from? He had nothing to apologize for.

Don't I?

He had brought her to Kyr against her will, but what choice did he have? She could be pregnant with his child. Until he knew for certain, he was not about to let her stay in America, living alone and working. What if something happened? What if her store was robbed or someone broke into her apartment?

He'd seen how flimsy her door locks were. Oh, she thought they were state-of-the-art, no doubt, but he'd hired some of the best lock pickers in existence when he'd been building his business from scratch. He'd wanted to test his security, and he knew how easily locks could be breached.

If someone wanted to get to her, they could. And if it became known that she might carry an heir to the throne of Kyr? He shuddered to think of it.

"You will not do anything so foolish again, Miss Sloane."

"I don't intend to—but I also don't want a companion. I want my freedom to come and go from this room, to talk to whomever I want to. And I want to talk to you from time to time. If there's a baby, then I want to know its father as something more than an arrogant stranger. And if there isn't, then I'll go home and forget I ever met you."

Rashid stood stiffly and stared down at her sitting there like some sort of tiny potentate. She had nerve, this woman. But it was absolutely out of the question. He wanted nothing to do with her. If she was pregnant, he'd deal with it when the time came—he could hardly think the word *wife*—but for now she was safely stowed away and he could go about business and forget she existed.

"You may come and go if that is what you wish. But you will have a servant to guide you, and you will do what you are told. You will not wear that clothing, Miss Sloane. You will dress as a Kyrian woman and you will be respectful."

Her chin lifted again. "I am always respectful of those who are respectful of me. But I refuse to be swathed head to toe in black robes—"

His anger was swift as he cut her off. "Once more, you make dangerous assumptions about us. I will send a seamstress to you and you may choose your own colors. This is nonnegotiable."

Her mouth flattened for the barest moment. And then her lips were lush and pink again as she nibbled the bottom one. “And am I to see you, too? Have conversations with you that aren’t about what I’m wearing or where I plan to live?”

He almost said yes. The word hovered on his tongue and he bit it back. Shock coursed through him at that near slip. Why would he want to spend any time with her? Why would he ever do such a thing? It was not in him. It was not what he did, regardless that he’d thought of that kiss for half the night during the flight home. He’d told himself it had simply been too long since he’d been with a woman and that was why he kept thinking about it.

But this woman was not the one he was going to break his fast with. That road was fraught with too many dangers. Too many complications.

“I think that is unnecessary,” he said curtly. “I have a kingdom to run and very little time.”

“I think it *is* necessary.” Her voice was soft and filled with a hurt he didn’t understand.

He refused to let her get to him. She was a stranger, a vessel who might be carrying his child. He did not care for her. He would not care for her.

“Yet this, too, is nonnegotiable,” he told her before turning and striding from the room.

CHAPTER FIVE

SHERIDAN DIDN'T KNOW why it hurt so much to watch him walk out, but it did. She didn't care about him at all—she actively disliked him, in fact—but his rejection stung. She might be carrying his child and he didn't even care about who she was as a person. He didn't want to know her, and he didn't seem to want her to know him.

She didn't move when the workmen came back inside to continue cleaning the glass, or when Fatima—the woman who'd brought her food and had returned after Sheridan broke the window—came over and took the cloth from her to wipe the remaining cuts. They were small, but they stung.

Oh, she'd been so stupid. So emotional. She'd behaved crazily—but it had worked because he'd come. And he'd promised her a small measure of freedom. That had to be a triumph. Fatima dabbed some ointment on her cuts, and then disappeared into the bathroom to put everything away.

How had it come to this? Sheridan was a nice person. She was friendly to everyone, she loved talking to people and she'd never met anyone she didn't like. Until yesterday when Rashid al-Hassan had shown up, she hadn't even thought it was possible to dislike someone.

There were people she got mad at, certainly. She got mad at Annie for not being stronger, but that only made her feel guilty. Annie hadn't had all the advantages that Sheridan had—she wasn't as outgoing, she hadn't been popular, she didn't know how to talk to people and make friends and now she couldn't even have a baby—so it was wrong of Sheridan to get angry with her. Sheridan could hear her mother's answer when she'd been a teen complaining that it wasn't fair she had to stay home from the party because her friends hadn't invited Annie, too.

Annie's not like you, Sheri. We have to be gentle with her. We have to watch out for her.

Not for the first time, Sheridan wondered if maybe Annie would be tougher if everyone in her life hadn't coddled her. If she'd had to stand up for herself, make her own friends, fight her own battles.

Sheridan clenched her hand into a fist and sat there as still as a statue for what seemed the longest time. Even now, she felt like she should be calling Annie to ask how she was instead of worrying about her own situation.

She looked up to see yet more men arriving in her room. They chattered in fast, musical Arabic, dragging out measuring tapes and writing things down on paper. Then they disappeared.

Everything transpired quickly and efficiently over the next couple of hours. Sheridan didn't see the new glass going in because by that time she was in her bedchamber—seriously, it was a chamber, not a bedroom—with three seamstresses, several bolts of fabric and ready-made samples hanging from a portable rack. A young woman who spoke English had come along to translate.

"This one, miss?"

Sheridan looked at the satiny peach fabric and felt a rush of pleasure. "Definitely."

The clothing the women wore was beautiful. Sheridan felt another wash of heat roll through her as she thought about her preconceived notions. She'd expected they would wear black burkas covering them from head to foot, but that was not at all the case.

The garments these women wore were colorful, lightweight and beautiful. They were long, modestly fitted dresses with embroidery and beading on the necks and bodices. The hijab, or head covering, was optional. Two of the women wore them and two did not.

But the possibilities there were beautiful, as well. The fabric was gossamer, colorful and draped in such a way that it created a sense of mystery and beauty.

The women worked quickly, draping bolts of fabric over her body, slipping pins inside and pulling the fabric away only to replace it with a new bolt. Sheridan tried on two dresses they had on the rack—one a gorgeous coral and the other a pretty shade of lavender that brought out the color of her eyes. The seamstress in charge promised they could have those two ready in a matter of hours once they returned to their shop and got to work. The others would take a full day.

Sheridan didn't want to imagine that she needed many dresses for her stay, but how could she know for certain?

The women packed everything up and left just as two men came in with Fatima. They were carrying a box with a flat-screen television in it and they proceeded to set it up on one of the credenzas nearest the bed.

Sheridan wandered into the living area of the suite and found a new television there, too, as well as a state-of-the-art computer and a newly installed telephone. The new glass was set into the casement and the men were sweeping up.

Her throat grew tight. Rashid had done what he'd promised. Thus far. He'd seemed surprised she'd had no television or computer, and he'd worked fast to correct it. But, as nice as this was, she'd wanted more from him. She'd wanted *his* time, wanted to understand more about this man who might just be the father of her baby. He could not be wholly unlikable, could he?

But he seemed determined not to give it to her.

She picked up the remote and flipped on the television. The one in the living area was mounted to the wall, and it was huge—it was almost like having a movie screen when all the colors suddenly came to life and filled the surface. It didn't take too long to figure out how the satellite worked—and her throat tightened again as she landed on CNN International and English conversation filled her ears.

It was nice to hear, but it only brought home how alone she was here. How would she get through a week of this? Nine months of this?

Rashid had said she could come and go, but only with an escort and only when she had the proper clothing. Since she still didn't, she wouldn't attempt to leave her quarters yet. She'd already behaved abominably.

She could still see him standing there, looking at her with the most furious expression on his face. He'd also, for a moment, seemed not fearful…but, well, something besides angry. Maybe *wary* was the word. Like he didn't want to be in the same room with her, but knew he had to be.

It hit her then that not only was he not attracted to her, but she also revolted him. He was tall and handsome and kingly, and she was a short blond woman who organized parties for people. She was pale and slight compared to him. He was the Lion of Kyr, or some such thing like that, and she was an ordinary house cat.

Who might just be pregnant with the next king of the jungle.

She would have laughed if it wasn't so serious. Sheridan went over to where Fatima had set a fresh pot of tea and some pastries and poured a cup. Despite the nausea, which came and went, she decided to try a pastry and see if it stayed down. After she'd made an impulsive decision to throw the tray at the window, she'd not eaten any of the food that she'd carefully set aside to get to the tray. Things had happened so quickly after that and she hadn't had time.

Sheridan frowned as she nibbled on a pastry. Rashid was repulsed by her. It made sense, in a way, and it certainly explained the way he acted.

But then she thought of their kiss again, of the way it had slid down into her skin and made her want things she'd almost forgotten existed. Even now, the memory of it made her tremble. He'd slid his tongue into her mouth and she'd practically devoured him.

How embarrassing.

But she'd thought, dammit, at least for a minute anyway, that he'd been equally affected. He'd kissed her with such hunger, such passion, that she'd been swept up in the moment.

Yes, swept up enough so that he could carry her to the car before she managed to make a peep. Sheridan set the pastry down with disgust. He'd certainly known what he was doing. And she'd been just sensation deprived enough to let him.

"Miss?"

Sheridan looked up to find Fatima standing over her. The two men were leaving, carting the remnants of television and computer boxes with them.

"Yes?"

"Do you require anything else?"

That was a loaded question if ever she heard one. "Your English is good, Fatima."

"Thank you, miss. I studied in school."

"Have you worked in the palace long?"

"A few months."

"Do you know the king well?"

She shook her head. "No, miss. King Rashid, may Allah bless him, has come home again after many years away. We will prosper under his benevolent reign."

Sheridan wasn't going to laugh over that *benevolent reign* remark, though she wanted to. But she also felt a spark of curiosity. "Many years away?"

Fatima looked a little worried then. "I have heard this in the palace. I do not know for certain. If you will excuse me, miss. Unless you need something?" she added, her eyes wide and almost pleading with Sheridan not to ask anything more about Rashid.

"Thank you, but I'm fine," she replied, offering the woman a smile to reassure her.

Fatima curtsied and then hurried out of the room, closing the door behind her with one last fearful glance at Sheridan.

After a long day sorting through national problems, including one between two desert tribes arguing over who owned a water well, Rashid was glad to retire to his quarters. These rooms had once been his father's, but he'd gotten the decorators to work immediately so that they no longer bore any resemblance to the man who'd lived in them for thirty-seven years.

Gone were the ornate furnishings and narcissistic portraits, the statuary, the huge bed on a platform complete with heavy damask draperies. In their place, Rashid had asked for clean lines, comfortable furniture, paintings that didn't overwhelm with color or subject matter and breezy fabrics more in fitting with the desert. Certainly the desert was bitterly cold at night, but he didn't need damask draperies for that.

The palace had been modernized years ago and had working air and heat for those rare occasions when it was needed. Rashid slipped his headdress off and dropped it on a couch. Then he raked his hand through his hair and pulled out his phone. He stared at it for a long moment before he punched the button that would call up his favorites.

Kadir answered on the third ring. "Rashid, it's good to hear from you."

"*Salaam,* brother." He chewed the inside of his lip and stared off toward the dunes and the setting sun. It blazed bright orange as it sank like a stone. He'd debated for hours on whether or not to call Kadir. They weren't as close as they'd once been, and he found it hard to admit he needed people. "How are you?"

Kadir laughed. "Wonderful. Happy. Ecstatic."

"Marriage agrees with you." He tried not to let any bitterness slip into his voice, but he feared it did anyway. Still, Kadir took it like a blissfully happy man would: as the uninformed judgment of a bachelor.

"Apparently so. Emily keeps me on my toes. But she

forces me to eat kale, Rashid. Because it has micronutrients or some such thing, she says it's good for me."

"That doesn't sound so bad." It sounded horrible.

"She makes a healthy drink for breakfast. It's green. Looks disgusting, but thankfully doesn't taste as bad as it looks." He sighed. "I miss pancakes and bacon."

Rashid was familiar with pancakes, though he'd never developed a taste for them during the brief time he'd spent in America. He almost laughed, but then he thought of Daria cooking meals for him and swallowed. She used to make these wonderful savory pies from her native Ural Mountains. He'd loved them. He'd loved her.

Rashid swallowed. "I want you to build a skyscraper for me, Kadir."

He could practically hear Kadir's brain kick into gear. "You do? Is this a Kyrian project, or a personal one?"

"I need a building for Hassan Oil in Kyr. I want you to build it."

"Then I am happy to do so. Let me check the schedule and I'll see when we can come for a meeting."

"That would be good."

Kadir sighed, as if sensing there was more to the call. "I will come anyway, Rashid, if you wish it."

He did wish it. For the first time in a long time, he wanted a friend. And Kadir was the closest thing he had. But a lifetime of shutting people out was hard to overcome. He'd let in Daria, but look how that had turned out.

"Whenever you can make it is good. I'm busy with many things since you left."

"I'm sorry we didn't make the coronation. It was my intention, and then—"

"It's fine." He pulled in a breath. "Kadir, there is something I want to talk about."

"Then I will come immediately."

That Kadir would still do that, after everything that had passed between them, made an uncomfortable rush of feeling fill Rashid's chest. "No, that is not necessary. But there's a woman. A situation."

"A situation?" He could hear the confusion in his brother's voice.

Rashid sighed. And then he told Kadir what had happened—the sperm mix-up, the trip to America, the way he'd given Sheridan no choice but to return with him. Kadir was silent for a long moment. Rashid knew his brother was trying to grasp the ramifications of the situation. At any rate, he couldn't know half of why this unnerved Rashid so much. Rashid hadn't hidden his marriage to Daria, but he'd been living in Russia then and the information hadn't precisely filtered out.

And the baby? He did not talk of that to anyone.

"So she might be pregnant?"

The ice in his chest was brittle. "Yes."

"What will you do? Marry her?"

Rashid hated the way that single word ground into his brain. *Marry.* "I will have to, won't I? But once the child is born, she can leave him here and return to America."

Kadir blew out a breath. Rashid wondered for a moment if he might be laughing. But his voice, when he spoke, was even. "I don't know, Rashid. The American I married would put my balls in a vise before she agreed to such a thing. In fact, I think most women would."

"Not if you pay them enough to disappear."

Kadir might have groaned. Rashid wasn't certain, because his blood was rushing in his ears. "You could try. It would certainly make it easier with the council if she would agree to disappear afterward. If she's pregnant, they will have to accept her. But they won't like it."

Rashid growled. "I don't give a damn what the council likes."

And it was true. The council was old and traditional, but there were lines he would not allow them to cross. He was the king. They had power because he allowed it, not in spite of it. They wanted him to marry a Kyrian. But if he wanted to marry a dancing bear, he would. And if he wanted to marry an American girl, he would do that, too.

"At least be nice to the woman, Rashid. You *are* being nice to her, yes?"

"Of course I am." But a current of guilt sizzled through him. He could still see her eyes, so wide and wounded, looking up at him today when he'd told her there was no reason for them to spend time together. No reason to know each other.

And perhaps there wasn't. But the days were ticking down and they would soon know if she were pregnant. And then he would have to take her as his wife.

It made him want to howl.

"We will come for a visit soon," Kadir said. "Perhaps it would be good to have Emily there. The poor woman is probably confused and scared."

He didn't think Sheridan was all that scared. He could still see her standing up to him, spitting like a wet cat when he'd told her he would take the child and raise him in Kyr.

"I am nice to her," he said defensively. "She is my guest."

Kadir laughed softly. "Somehow, I don't think she sees it quite the same way."

They spoke for a few more minutes about other things, and then Rashid ended the call. He sighed and went out onto one of the many terraces that opened off his rooms. There was a soft breeze tonight, hot and scented with jasmine from the gardens. In another few hours, it would turn chilly, but for now it was still warm.

The minarets glowed ocher in the last rays of the setting sun. The sounds of vendors shouting in the streets filtered to him on the wind, along with the fresh scent of spicy meat and hot bread.

Rashid breathed it all in. This was home. Unbidden, an image of Sheridan Sloane came to mind. She had a home, too, and he'd forced her out of it. For her own protection, yes, but nevertheless she was here in a strange place and nothing was familiar.

Guilt pricked him. He should not care about her feelings at all, but if she was truly carrying his child, did he want her upset and stressed? Wasn't it better to make her welcome?

He sighed again, knowing what he had to do. Tomorrow, he would take lunch with her. They would talk, she would be happy and he would leave again, content in the knowledge he'd done his part.

It was only an hour—and he could be nice to anyone for an hour.

Sheridan awoke in the middle of the night. It was dark and still and she was cold. She sat up, intending to pull the blanket up from the bottom of the bed, but she wasn't all that tired now. Her sleep was erratic because of the time difference. She checked her phone for the time—

still no signal—and calculated that it was midafternoon at home. She never napped during the day, so it was no wonder she was messed up.

She got up and pulled on her silky robe over her nightgown before going into the bathroom. Hair combed, teeth brushed, she wandered into the living area. And then, because she was curious, she went and opened the door to her suite. The guard was not there. She stood there for a moment in shock, and then she crept into the corridor.

She didn't know where she was going or what she expected, but she kept moving along, thinking someone would stop her at any moment. But no one did. The corridors were quiet, as if everyone was asleep. She didn't know how it usually worked in palaces, but it made sense they were all in bed.

When she reached the end of a corridor and came up against a firmly locked door, she turned and went back the way she'd come. There were doors off the corridor, and she tentatively opened one. It was a space with seating, but it wasn't quite as ornate as hers. It was, not plain precisely, but modern. Personally, she preferred some antiques, but this space was intended for someone who liked little fuss.

She thought perhaps she'd stumbled into a meeting area since it was so sterile. A breeze came in through doors that were open to the night air and she headed toward them. She hadn't been outside since she'd arrived, and she wondered what it would be like in the desert at night.

She stepped onto a wide terrace. The city lights spread out around her and, in the distance, the darkness of the desert was like a crouching tiger waiting for an excuse to pounce. She moved to the railing and stood, gripping it and sucking in the clean night air. It was chilly now, which amazed her considering how hot it had been when she'd arrived.

A frisson of excitement dripped down her spine. It surprised her, but in some ways it didn't. She'd never been to the desert before. Never been to an Arab country with dunes and palaces and camels and men who wore headdresses and robes. It was foreign, exotic and, yes, exciting in a way. She wanted to explore. She wanted to ride a horse into that desert and see what was out there.

She heard a noise behind her, footsteps across tile, and she whirled with her heart in her throat. How would she explain her presence here to her guard? To anyone?

But it wasn't just anyone standing there. It was a man she recognized on a level that stunned her. Rashid al-Hassan stood in a shaft of light, his chest and legs bare. He looked like an underwear model, she thought crazily, all lean muscle and golden flesh. He was not soft—not that she'd expected he would be after he'd pressed her against him—but the corrugated muscle over his abdomen was a bit of a sensual shock. Real men weren't supposed to look like that.

"What are you doing here, Miss Sloane?" he demanded, his voice hard and cold and so very dangerous.

The warmth that had been undulating through her like a gentle wave abruptly shut off.

Run! That was the single word that echoed in her brain.

But she couldn't move. Her limbs were frozen. Not only that, but Rashid al-Hassan also stood between her and escape….

CHAPTER SIX

SHERIDAN SUCKED IN a deep breath and pulled her robe tighter, even though it couldn't protect her from the fury in his dark eyes. She thought of Fatima's fearful look earlier today and wondered if perhaps this man was more frightening than she'd thought. Her blood ran cold.

"The door was open. I—I wanted to see outside."

"You are in my quarters, Miss Sloane."

Oh, dear. "I'm sorry. I didn't know."

He still hadn't moved. He stood in the door, his broad frame imposing. She told herself not to look below the level of his chin. She failed.

"So you decided to wander in the middle of the night and open random doors?"

She twisted the tie of her robe. "Something like that. I'm on a different schedule than you, I'm afraid. Wide-awake and nothing to do."

"Nothing to do." His voice was somehow full of meaning. Or perhaps she imagined it.

"I didn't mean to disturb you."

He still looked imposing and impossible. And then he shoved his hand through his hair and moved out of the doorway and onto the terrace. Sheridan stood frozen.

"You didn't disturb me. I was awake."

"You should try hot milk. It helps with insomnia." Oh, no, she was babbling. Sheridan bit her lip and told herself to shut up. This man was dangerous, for heaven's sake. Not at all the sort to put up with babbling in the middle of the night.

"I don't need much sleep," he said. "And I don't like hot milk."

"I don't either, actually. But I understand it works for some."

He went and leaned on the railing, near her. She thought she should take this opportunity to escape, and yet she was curious enough to want to stay. He made her nerves pop and sing. It was an interesting sensation.

"When it's light, you can see all the way to the gulf from here," he said. He lifted his hand. "In that direction, you can see the dunes of the Kyrian Desert. The Waste is out there, too."

"The Waste?" She moved closer, reached for the railing and wound her fingers around the iron.

He turned his head toward her. "A very harsh, very hot part of the desert. There is no water for one hundred miles. The sands are baked during the day, and at night they give up their heat and turn cool. You can freeze out there, if you don't die of heatstroke during the day."

It was hard to imagine such a place in this day and age. "Surely there are ways to bring water into it."

"There are. But there is no reason to do so. It would be cost prohibitive, for one thing. And who would live there? There are nomads, but the people who are accustomed to the cities would never go."

"Have you been there?"

He didn't speak for a long moment. "I have. There is an oasis midway. It was once part of a trade route across the desert. I went as a boy. It was part of my training as an al-Hassan."

She could imagine this harsh, dark man out there now. But as a child? It seemed so dangerous and uncertain. "I've never been to a desert before. I've never been anywhere but the Caribbean. Until now, I mean."

He looked at her. "Are you more comfortable now that you have a television and internet access?"

"It helps. But I'm still used to doing more than I have the last day. I like to be busy."

"Consider it a vacation."

"That would be easier if it actually were."

"Miss Sloane—"

"Sheridan. Please." Because she felt so out of place when he called her Miss Sloane. She needed him to acknowledge her as more than a random stranger. Because, regardless of whether or not there was a baby, they'd shared something incredibly intimate. Even if it had been clinical.

"Sheridan."

She shivered at the sound of her name on his lips. Why? Because it sounded like a silken caress. "Thank you," she said.

"I was going to say that I realize this is not easy for you. It is not easy for me, either."

"I know."

He turned to look out at the city lights and she watched the play of the wind in his hair and the soft glow of moonlight on his profile. He was a very beautiful man. And a lonely one. She didn't know why she thought he was lonely, but she did.

"I have decided to give you what you've requested," he said, and her heart thrummed. "I want your stay to be pleasant. If it pleases you to talk to me, then I will grant it."

She was surprised and pleased at once. "I appreciate that very much."

They stood there in silence for a long moment. "It is an extraordinary length to go to, to have a baby for someone else."

She felt a touch defensive. "It's not just for anyone. Annie is my sister."

"I am aware of this."

Sheridan sighed. The night breeze whipped up then, just for a moment, and she shivered. "She and Chris have tried and tried. They've seen doctors and been through one treatment after another. Nothing seems to work." She gripped the railing tightly, staring off toward the flickering lights of the city. "There was one doctor who mentioned an experimental treatment in Europe. Annie wanted to do it, and Chris would do anything for her. But the cost… Well, it's a lot. And there are no guarantees. They would have to sell everything and then hope…" She swallowed the lump in her throat. "I offered to step in before they went deeper into debt."

"So you would put your own life on hold to have this child for your sister. And then you would hand him or her over as if the previous nine months had happened to her instead of you."

The lump in her throat wouldn't go away. She hugged her arms around herself to keep from shivering. The air seemed colder now. "I didn't say it would be easy, but it's what you do when you love someone. You make sacrifices."

He seemed very quiet and still as he watched her. She'd expected him to make some sort of remark, but he said nothing at all. It began to worry her, though she didn't quite know why. She cleared her throat softly and told him the truth.

"I don't quite know what to say to you," she admitted. "I never know if you're angry or if you're just the kind of man who doesn't speak much."

He was looking at her with renewed interest. "I'm not angry. I'm frustrated."

"We're both frustrated."

"Are we?"

"I…" She sensed that this conversation had moved out of her control somehow. His eyes glittered in the night. He seemed suddenly very intense. And very—dear heaven—*naked.* "Yes, uh, of course. Why wouldn't we be? This is a frustrating circumstance."

"I find it very interesting that you could be carrying my child, and yet we've never been intimate. I've never undressed you, never tasted your skin."

She was growing hot now. So very hot. "Well, er…"

"Have you thought of it, Sheridan? After that kiss, have you wondered?"

Her heart hammered hard. Another moment and she would be dizzy. Yes she'd thought of that kiss. And she'd thought of her flesh pressed against his, nothing between them but skin and heat. She'd wondered what it would be like to be this man's lover. This dynamic, incredible man.

"Of course I have," she said, shocking herself with the admission. And him, too, if the way his muscles seemed to coil tight beneath his skin was any indication. He was like a great cat ready to pounce. The Lion of Kyr, indeed. "But that doesn't mean I want to do anything about it."

Liar.

"Then I think perhaps you should be more careful which rooms you wander into in the middle of the night."

His voice was icy again, yet it was somehow hot, too. Not menacing, but promising in a way that had her limbs quivering.

"I didn't know this was your room. And I didn't come here for…for…"

She couldn't finish the sentence. Her ears were hot, which was ridiculous because she wasn't a naive virgin. She hadn't had many lovers—well, only two, in fact—but that didn't mean she didn't know what happened when a man and a woman got naked together.

But it was the imagining that was killing her here. Rashid was beautiful, dark and dangerous and mysterious, and the idea of him completely focused on her body was more arousing than she could have imagined possible. She reminded herself that she didn't like him, but her body didn't seem to care. *So what?* That was the message throbbing in her sex, her veins, her belly. A relentless throb of tension and yearning that would only be broken if this man took her to his bed.

"Perhaps you did not," he said smoothly, "but you want it nevertheless. I can see it in your eyes, Sheridan."

She tried to stiffen in outrage. She was fully aware her nipples had beaded tight against the silk of the robe. Instead of trying to hide them, she wrapped her arms beneath her breasts and hugged herself against the chill air. Not that she was all that cold with Rashid al-Hassan looking at her like he might devour her. Which was a bit of a shock since she'd convinced herself that he wasn't really attracted to her.

Apparently she was wrong….

"You're being too polite, Rashid. You mean to say you can see it in my nipples, but the truth is it's cold out here," she said brazenly. "It has nothing to do with you."

"I'm not the kind of man one issues challenges to, *habibti*. I have a pathological need to prove the issuer wrong."

She took a step backward. "We don't know each other well enough. Touch me and I'll scream."

He laughed. It was completely unexpected. She didn't like the warmth dripping into her limbs at the sound. "You forget this is the royal palace of Kyr and I am the king. If I wish to tie you to my bed and have my way with you on a nightly basis, there is no one who will stop me."

Her heart hammered. She wasn't supposed to be titillated by the idea of being tied to Rashid's bed. And yet she was.

He moved then, toward her, and she didn't even try to get away. She was frozen like a gazelle, waiting for the big cat to strike. And strike he did. He tugged her against him, her body in the thin silk robe flush to his naked flesh, and spread his hands over her backside.

Yet he didn't hold her tight. She could escape if she wished. She knew it and he knew it—and she didn't even try.

He laughed again, softly, triumphantly. "Such a liar, Sheridan," he said thickly. And then his mouth came down on hers.

If the kiss in her store had been surprising in its intensity, this one was downright earth-shattering. Rashid's tongue traced the seam of her lips and she opened to him, tangling her tongue with his almost eagerly.

The sensations rioting through her were more intense than she ever recalled experiencing before. It was the hormones from the shots, she told herself—but it was also the man. He was more exciting than anyone she'd ever known. Which didn't make any sense because he was also the least likable person she'd ever known.

Not to mention she didn't even really know him at all. He was a king, a desert sheikh, an autocratic ruler accustomed to ordering people around and getting his way.

And she was giving him precisely what he expected.

But it felt so good. Their tongues fought a blistering duel, her skin grew moist and impossibly hot and wetness flooded her sex. Her limbs were weakened by the kiss and she lifted her arms to put them around his neck. The shock of his hot skin beneath hers made her whimper.

Rashid turned her until her back was against the railing—and then he untied her robe and slipped it off her shoulders. The next thing she knew, his hot mouth was tracing a path down the column of her throat while she threaded her fingers into his dark hair and clutched him to her.

His teeth bit down on her nipple through the silken fabric of her nightgown and she gasped. It wasn't a hard bite, but it had the effect of sending pleasure shooting straight to her core. Her body clenched hard with desire as she gripped his shoulders and thrust her breasts toward his mouth.

She wanted him to remove the thin tissue of silk between his mouth and her body, but he didn't. He licked her through the fabric, nibbled and sucked until she was wild with need. Her nipples were more sensitive than ever since she'd had the hormone shots. If he did nothing but this all night, she knew she would come from the stimulation.

But he had no intention of doing only that. He reached down and gathered the hem of her nightie, lifting it up her legs, exposing her. Sheridan thought she needed to protest, but some needy, wicked part of her really didn't want to.

Rashid's hands glided beneath her gown, up the flesh of her abdomen, until he was cupping her breasts beneath the fabric, his hot hands spanning her skin, making it burn.

His mouth claimed hers again. It wasn't a tender kiss, or even a teasing kiss. It was a full-out assault on her senses. He stepped in closer, pinning her body to the railing with his much bigger, much harder one.

And that was when she felt him. That insistently hard part of him that pressed into her, letting her know that he was every bit as affected by the tension and heat between them as she was.

Sheridan acted instinctively. She reached for him, cupped her hands over that hard part of him she shouldn't crave but did. It had been so long since she'd been with anyone and she was suddenly ravenous. Rashid made a noise, a growl of satisfaction or encouragement in his throat. A thrill shot through her.

She'd thought he'd be disgusted by her, but that clearly wasn't the case. He wanted her. And, right now, she wanted him. It was insane, but nothing about this situation was normal. If she slept with him, what would change? Not a damn thing.

She pushed her hands beneath his briefs, cupped him in her hands. He was big and full and so very ready that it almost scared her. She didn't know this man at all, and what she did know hadn't been very pleasant up until this point.

He'd threatened her, taken her against her will and brought her here and treated her as if she was someone he'd hired to do a job instead of a woman caught up in a mistake not of her own making. He'd been angry with her, and he'd started this to prove a point, to punish her.

Now he was in her hands, his body hard and taut and ready. He broke the kiss and stared down at her, his eyes dark and deep and so fathomless she was almost frightened. But he was just a man, she reminded herself, and he'd not harmed her. He'd never given a single indication that he would force her to do anything she didn't want to do.

"Sheridan," he growled, his voice as tight as she'd yet heard it. "If you don't mean to give yourself to me, you need to leave. Now. Because if you continue to touch me like that, I'm not stopping until I've tasted you as thoroughly as I desire."

Sheridan bit her lip as her heart skittered recklessly in her chest. A sane woman would leave right this instant. A sane woman would not give her body to a man she barely knew simply because he made her feel more excited than she'd ever felt before.

She was not precisely sane at this moment. Maybe it was the heat of the desert, or the sand, or the opulent palace. She had no idea, but she wanted things she shouldn't want.

"I don't want to leave. I don't want to stop touching you."

With a groan, he swept her up into his arms and carried her through the door.

CHAPTER SEVEN

SOMEWHERE ON THE trip to his bed, panic began to flood her system. But before she could react, he set her on the bed and stripped her nightgown from her body. And then he was hovering over her, kissing her until her fear melted and her body caught on fire again.

Oh, this was so wrong—and so right. Sheridan put her arms around him, ran her hands over his broad back, the thick muscles and tendons, down his biceps and over his pecs. He was magnificent, and he no doubt knew it.

He left her mouth to lick his way to her breasts again. He took his time, sliding his tongue around and around before he sucked one aching nipple into his mouth. Sheridan cried out with the intensity of the pleasure spiking through her.

"You are sensitive," he murmured, his breath hot against her skin and yet cold where it drifted over her wet nipple. "So sensitive."

Sheridan couldn't speak. Her stomach churned with anticipation and, yes, even fear. Because what was she doing? Part of her brain kept wondering, but the rest refused to entertain any alternatives to what was currently happening.

And then Rashid moved down her body, his hands

spanning her hips and peeling her panties down until he pulled them free and dropped them somewhere on the floor. She could see his beautiful face illuminated by moonlight, see the vaulted ceilings of the chamber, hear the exotic sounds of the Kyrian night drifting inside—and it made her feel as if she wasn't herself. As if this was a fantasy. A thousand and one Arabian nights with her own desert king.

Sheridan bowed up off the bed as he touched his mouth to the wet seam of her body. The pleasure was so intense, so spellbinding, that she practically sobbed his name. He gave her no relief from the feelings rocketing through her. He held her legs open and licked her until she was a shuddering mass of nerve endings.

Sheridan's world exploded in a white-hot blaze of light, her body tightening almost painfully before soaring over the edge. But before she could manage to come back to herself, Rashid was there, his mouth capturing hers, demanding her full attention. She melted into his kiss.

And then she felt him, big and hard and poised at her body's entrance. He put a hand under her bottom, lifted her toward him. She wrapped her legs around him, her heart pounding as she waited for what happened next.

He seemed to hesitate for a long moment. And then he said something in Arabic, some muttered phrase, before he pushed into her body. He didn't move fast, didn't jam himself inside her. He took his time. And then he was deep within her, the two of them joined in the most intimate of ways, and fresh panic began to unwind inside her belly.

What was she doing? What was wrong with her? Sex with a stranger wasn't like her at all!

Rashid's head dropped slowly toward hers and she closed her eyes, tilting her mouth up until he captured it. She sighed—or maybe that was him. But then he started to move and she no longer cared about anything except what he was doing to her.

He was gentle at first. But as she arched her body into his, he took her harder and harder, until they were moving into each other in an almost punishing rhythm. She ran her hands over his skin until he gripped her wrists and shoved her hands over her head, binding her.

It was erotic, sensual and utterly exhilarating. Their skin grew hot and moist as they tangled together and the tension inside her coiled tighter than the lid on a pressure cooker.

And then she couldn't hold on a moment longer. He was too good at this, too compelling, and she came in a rush of blinding intensity that left her gasping for air and crying his name at the same time.

She felt his body tighten inside hers, and then he flew over the edge with her, his breath a harsh groan in her ear. They lay together for a few moments, hearts pounding, skin slicked with perspiration, breaths razoring in and out. Sheridan's legs trembled from gripping his hips so tightly with her thighs. She eased them down and lay still beneath him, her eyes closed and her brain finally began to whir into consciousness again.

What did one say after sex like that? Especially with a man you hardly knew and definitely didn't like?

She didn't get a chance to find out.

He pushed off her and stood, and cool air wafted over her skin, chilling her. She wanted to grab the covers and pull them up, and yet she couldn't seem to move. Because he was staring down at her, his face stark in the darkness, his chest rising and falling with more than exertion.

He was angry. Or tormented. She wasn't sure which, and it alarmed her. She sat up and wrapped her arms around her knees, trying to hide herself.

"Thank you, Sheridan," he said, his voice so courteous and calm. And cold. Sheridan shivered at the frost in his tone. He bent down a moment and then straightened, laying her nightgown and underwear on the bed at her feet. "Get dressed and I will escort you back to your room."

Rashid was up at dawn. He'd tossed and turned for the past couple of hours in a bed that still smelled like the woman he'd shared it with. The corners of his mouth turned down in a frown as his stomach twisted with guilt.

But why should that be? He enjoyed sex as well as the next man. He'd only ever loved one woman with his heart, but he'd loved many women in the physical way. He was not a monk and he hadn't been celibate for the past five years. It had taken him over a year to take a woman to his bed again, but he'd done so.

Sex with Sheridan Sloane was nothing out of the ordinary for him. And yet it was. Because she might be carrying his child, and though he'd been so focused and intent on her body, on tasting her and enjoying her, he hadn't expected the gravity of that fact to hit him with such a jolt after he'd found his pleasure in her body.

He'd bedded the woman who could be pregnant with his heir. A woman he didn't love, but who he would have to take as his wife if she was.

Still, he should be happy he'd finally released some

of this pent-up tension. He was not. He was strangely restless. Keyed up.

Ready to explore Sheridan's creamy skin and secret recesses again and again.

That was the part that unnerved him. The sex had been pretty spectacular, hot and exciting and intense, and he'd been utterly focused on it, lost in it.

But then it was over and they'd lain there together, breathing hard, her heart throbbing against his own—and he'd wanted to escape. He didn't understand how he could be so cold and unemotional one minute and so gutted the next.

She'd gutted him. Sex with her had gotten into his head in a way that sex with other women did not—and he didn't like it one bit. So he'd risen and gone to get her robe from the terrace while she dressed. When he'd come back, he'd handed it to her silently. It had been cold from being outdoors, but she'd put it on anyway and belted it tight.

Then he'd escorted her back to her quarters because he hadn't been certain she could find her way alone. She hadn't spoken on the walk back down the corridors. He'd stopped in front of the door to the women's quarters, vowing to himself to station a guard there at night in the future instead of outside the entrance to the private wing.

There was another way to her rooms, through his own, but he'd refused to use it. It would be too easy to go through that entry again if he started now, so he simply didn't.

She'd hesitated at the door as if she wanted to say something to him, but he'd put his hands in her hair and held her face up for his kiss. To silence her. To end any awkwardness.

When she'd been rubbery and clinging to him, when his body was beginning to respond with fresh heat that he knew would ignite into a fire at any moment, he'd let her go, striding away without another word.

Her reaction had been a very resounding door slam. But it was for the best, really. He had too much to do, too many things to worry about, and no time to navigate the mire of repeatedly bedding a woman who might be carrying his heir. A woman who might soon be his wife.

If she was angry with him, so much the better. He'd intended to be nice to her, but he'd gone way overboard. And now he would have to stay away from her, as he'd intended in the first place.

Sheridan didn't believe that Rashid would come to see her that day. After the confusing—and paradigm changing—previous night, she didn't really think his decision to talk to her would stand.

And of course she was right. As the day wore into night, there was no sign of Rashid. She was allowed to wander the palace, as he'd promised, but she did not bump into him anywhere. She wore one of the dresses from the dressmaker, along with a hijab that covered her hair, and then she spent fascinating hours walking through the palace and studying the architecture.

But in spite of her enjoyment of everything the palace had to offer, she remained preoccupied with Rashid. With last night. She couldn't think of it without blushing. She'd had sex with him—hot, wild, crazy, passionate sex—after knowing him for two days.

Worse, she wanted more. She knew it wasn't going to

happen—that it *shouldn't* happen—but she couldn't help but imagine Rashid coming to her room in the night. He would peel her clothing away, and then use that magical mouth of his to drive her insane with wild need.

Sheridan fanned herself absently with her hand. The guard who strode silently along wherever she went didn't bat an eyelash. She'd tried to talk to him about mundane things, but he remained silent.

When she ventured out to the stables after dinner, he followed. But when she tried to touch one of the horses, just to pet its velvety nose, he stopped her.

"His Majesty would not want you to get bitten, miss."

"I've been around horses before," she said, more than a little surprised that he spoke English. She'd started to think he was ignoring her because he didn't speak her language. "I think I can tell when they're going to bite."

Still, she strolled along until they came to a room at the end of the stable. She looked over the top of the door and practically melted.

"Puppies!" She turned to her guard. "What kind of dogs are they?"

He seemed to hesitate, as if he didn't want to engage in conversation, but then he relented. "They are Canaan dogs, miss. A hardy and ancient breed."

The puppies were small and squat, and had curled tails. They almost looked like huskies, except they weren't gray and didn't have thick fur. The mother dog was nowhere to be seen at the moment.

"They're precious."

Sheridan stood and watched the puppies wiggling happily, playing and yipping, and wished she could go in and sit down and let them climb all over her. But she knew her guard wouldn't approve of that. Eventually, the sound of approaching hoofbeats made her turn her head. A man in desert robes sat astride a beautiful bay horse as it trotted toward the stable. When they reached the building, he swung down and handed the reins to a groom, who had appeared out of nowhere.

And then the man turned his head until dark glittering eyes met hers, boring into her with that combination of heat and anger that seemed unique to Rashid. Her belly clenched at the primal recognition that stirred to life inside her.

Beside her, her guard had dropped into a low bow. Sheridan, not quite knowing what to do, decided to curtsy. Oh, she was plenty angry with Rashid, but she would not create trouble by refusing to acknowledge his power over his subjects. She wasn't stupid and she knew it was important to have her guard's respect.

Rashid's eyes narrowed—and then he came toward her. His gaze raked over her, taking in the hijab and dress—which she'd realized weren't strictly necessary since she'd seen women in his palace dressed in Western business attire—before landing on her face again.

"Miss Sloane, isn't it a bit late to be touring the stables?"

Miss Sloane. As if he hadn't been inside her just a few hours ago. She lifted her chin. "I believe I already established that I'm still on a different sleep schedule than Kyr. Though it isn't quite eight o'clock here yet, which I would consider early even were I acclimated to your time zone."

Her heart thundered relentlessly in her breast as she stared at him. He was no longer quite the stranger he'd been before last night's passionate encounter, and it disconcerted her.

He turned his attention to the guard. "Leave us."

The guard rose and melted into the night. Sheridan felt a hot wash of anger move through her.

"I realize you're a king, but do you have to talk to people like that?"

His brows drew down. "Like what? I told him what he needed to know. Do you prefer I ask him politely to go?"

"It might be nice, but no, I don't really expect that out of you."

"You sound like my brother."

She blinked. "Do I? Is he a nice, sensible man?"

"Nicer than I am."

"So you admit you aren't very nice."

"I'm not trying to be." He shrugged. "I am who I am. I don't have to explain myself to anyone."

She dropped her gaze. It was an odd conversation in some respects. Odd because of what they'd done the night before, and odd because she could feel that fire beneath the surface. It was only waiting for ignition.

"After last night, I really didn't expect an explanation."

Oh, wow, had she really said that? She wanted to bite her tongue.

He searched her features. "You are upset because I did not allow you to stay in my bed."

"Allow?" She resisted the urge to poke him in the chest, but only barely. "What makes you think I wanted to stay? We were finished and it would have been awkward to stay. You don't strike me as the type for small talk, and I'd rather not have to attempt it. It was better that I left."

His dark eyes flashed with some unidentifiable emotion. "You continually surprise me. I thought you would be upset. Regretful. Wringing your hands and wishing you could undo the things we did together."

She shrugged as if casual sex was her thing when it really wasn't. "Why would I want to undo it? It was nice."

"Nice?" His voice was a growl and she suddenly wanted to laugh. Even superior kings had fragile egos when it came to their performance in bed. Hint that you were less than satisfied and you found yourself faced with a dangerously tense male animal with a point to prove.

"Unlike *you,* yes, it was nice. Very nice, if you insist."

He stiffened. And then he laughed softly. Once more, the sound of his laughter had a way of surprising her. It was as if he didn't laugh often enough and wasn't quite sure how. "You are baiting me. I see it now. If I said the moon was golden tonight, you'd say it was yellow."

That pesky warmth was flowing in her limbs again. Her body ached with his nearness, and though she had another, more immediate ache between her thighs to remind her of his possession, that didn't stop her from wanting it again.

"And what am I supposed to be baiting you into?" Her voice was huskier than she would have liked it. But he already knew how he affected her. One corner of his mouth lifted in a superior grin.

"Perhaps you want another demonstration of my niceness."

Heat flooded her cheeks. "Hardly. Once was enough, thank you."

Once was not enough. And that really worried her. Why did she want him? It wasn't like her to crave a man the way she craved him after only one night. Plus, this was too complicated. They weren't dating. This wasn't a man she'd met in Savannah, a man with the freedom and ability to pursue a relationship with her.

This was a king. A man who ruled a desert nation. A man who was so unlike any man she'd ever known that he confused her. He was arrogant, bossy and he already acted as if he owned her.

And she *let* him. She'd always thought she was a feminist, but the way he made her behave was decidedly not liberated. It was needy, physical and completely focused on sexual pleasure. If he threw her into a stall right now and had his way with her on the hay, she'd only urge him on.

He moved away from her and she tried not to let her disappointment show.

"Come, I will take you back to your quarters."

She threw another glance at the puppies before joining him. They walked side by side, but not touching, toward the palace.

"You like puppies?" he said.

"I love puppies. I've never had a dog, but I plan to get one some day."

"You've never had a dog?"

She shook her head as they walked across the courtyard. "My sister was bitten by a neighbor's dog when she was four. So we never got one because she was too scared."

"That hardly seems fair," he said.

Sheridan felt that old familiar prick of resentment flaring deep inside. It was followed, as always, by guilt. It wasn't Annie's fault.

"Maybe not, but she cried whenever my parents

talked about getting a dog for the family, so they gave up. We didn't even have a cat."

"Did a cat bite her, too?"

Sheridan stopped abruptly. Rashid was a few steps ahead when he turned toward her, waiting. "She had allergies," Sheridan said. "And it's not her fault."

He moved toward her again. She had to tilt her head back to look up at him. He bristled with a coiled energy that she was certain contained a hint of anger. At her? At Annie?

"Perhaps not, but it seems to me as if your sister's problems have done nothing but impact your life. Did you always give up everything you wanted for her sake?"

Sheridan's chest grew tight. The lump in her throat was huge. "Don't talk to me that way. You don't know my sister and you have no right to judge her. Annie's fragile. She needs me."

His gaze raked her face. "Yes, she needs you. She needs you to acquiesce to her demands, to give her what she wants, to provide the thing she believes she's been cheated out of."

Sheridan gasped. And then she reacted. She moved to slap him, but he caught her wrist and held it tight. His dark eyes were hard. And filled with a sympathy she'd not seen there before.

She was shaking deep inside. "How dare you? Annie didn't ask me to have this baby for her. I offered! And I'm going to do it, even if it takes another year to start again."

He ran his fingers down her cheek tenderly, and she trembled. "Of course you offered, *habibti*. Because you love her and because you were afraid for her. I don't fault you for this. I fault her for refusing to see what it might cost you."

She shook her head softly. "They are paying for the procedure and the birth. It's not costing me anything."

He let her go and stepped back. His mouth was a white line now. "It costs nine months of your life, it places a burden on your body and then there is the emotional impact of giving up the child at the end. That is not *nothing.*"

He was confusing her. Just a couple of days ago he'd suggested she turn over any child to him and now he was talking about the emotional impact of that kind of decision. Who was this man?

"I knew that when I offered."

His expression was black. "Yes, but did you also know that you were offering to risk your life? Did you consider that? Did she?"

Sheridan's heart pounded. "Childbirth is safe. This isn't the eighteenth century."

He stood stone-still but she sensed his muscles had coiled tight. As if he was a nuclear reaction waiting to happen. But then he pulled in a deep breath and huffed it out again and she knew he'd found the switch to turn it off.

"Of course it's not. You are correct."

Sheridan had a strong urge to reach for him, but she didn't. Something was bothering him. Some dark emotion reflected in his gaze, but she wasn't quite sure what it was.

"What's this about, Rashid?"

"It's not about anything," he finally said.

Her voice was little more than a whisper. "I don't believe you."

He stood there for a long moment, as if he was fighting an internal battle. And then he turned and strode away without another word, disappearing into the long gallery running along the back of the palace.

CHAPTER EIGHT

THE DAYS PASSED too slowly. Sheridan kept hoping to see Rashid, but he seemed to be avoiding her. She emailed with Kelly, planned the menus for two upcoming parties and felt guilty for not being there to help with the physical preparations. But there was really no need. Dixie Doin's operated like the efficient party machine it was meant to be.

Sheridan had spent a lot of time making sure that was so when she'd decided to have a baby for her sister. Though she'd intended to work until the birth, there were never any guarantees and she'd wanted to be prepared for anything.

Kelly hardly missed her, though she assured Sheridan that she missed her personally. Emails from Annie were another story. Sheridan dreaded to open them. She knew Annie was upset, but the lack of understanding about the situation made her stomach hurt. Her sister actively hoped that the IUI had failed. Sheridan understood that wish, understood it would be the easiest thing for them all. She'd thought the same thing when she'd first been told, but now that she was here with Rashid and he was real to her, not just a random sperm donor, the situation was much more complicated.

She thought of the man who had touched her so sensually, the man who heated her blood and chilled her bones and confused her to no end. No, this situation was no longer random and impersonal. It had ceased to be so the instant he'd walked into her life.

If Rashid hadn't come looking for her in Savannah, what would Annie have wanted her to do? Sheridan didn't want to know, and yet she couldn't help thinking about it. Would Annie have wanted this baby, too? Or would she have wanted Sheridan to terminate the pregnancy so she could start fresh with Chris's sperm?

She didn't even know if she was pregnant yet, but already she was emotional over the idea of losing this baby. Would it have been simpler if she'd never met Rashid, never slept with him?

Probably, but it was too late for that.

Sheridan took her usual route through the palace, stopping in the kitchen to see the staff and find out what they were preparing. She was fascinated with the food here, the fresh olive oil and breads, the fruits and nuts, and the flavorful dishes made with chicken and goat. The staff seemed wary at first, but as her visits increased—and Daoud, her formerly silent guard, or Fatima translated for her—they began to look forward to her arrival.

She tasted food, oohed and aahed appropriately and discussed ingredients. She even made note of some things to try for Dixie Doin's. Not everything was Kyrian, however. There was plenty of French cuisine as well, which surprised her at first but not when she considered that the French had once sent colonists to Kyr.

If anyone found it odd that an American woman roamed the palace, they did not say so. In spite of the women she saw in business attire, she kept to the rules

Rashid had set and wore Kyrian clothing. She even wore the hijab, because when her blond hair was hidden people seemed less likely to see her as an outsider.

Not that all Kyrians had black hair—there were some brown and tawny gold heads she'd seen—but her hair was so pale as to be noticeable when uncovered.

She'd gone to see the puppies again. When there was no sign of the mother dog, she asked Daoud why. That was when she learned that the puppies were orphans. They were being bottle-fed and taken care of by the grooms. She'd had Daoud ask if she could feed them, though he'd seemed reluctant to let her.

But she'd done it, and then she'd found herself surrounded by yipping dogs while she giggled and petted them and watched them suck down the milk. They were so sweet and she loved spending time with them. It was the highlight of each day, especially as she never saw Rashid.

She thought about him. She lay in her bed at night with her hand over her belly and thought about the man she'd made love to only once. The man whose baby might be in her womb right now.

She wondered where he was, if he was in his own bed and thinking of her, or if that single night had been an aberration and he now gave her no more consideration than what he'd had for breakfast. Probably the latter, considering she hadn't seen him since that night when he'd left her standing in the darkened courtyard.

She'd considered walking down the corridor in the middle of the night again, opening his door and making him talk to her. But when she'd gotten brave enough to act on it, a guard had been stationed outside her own door. He'd looked up from his tablet computer, his eyes meeting hers steadily until she'd shut the door.

Clearly, Rashid had thought she might come looking for him and had taken steps to prevent it. She was somehow both embarrassed and furious at once at the notion.

Still, Sheridan went through the days and did not ask where Rashid was. If he thought she was pining for him, then she was going to prove she wasn't. How could she when he was still such a stranger?

An enigmatic, compelling stranger that she wanted to know better.

Soon it was the night before her pregnancy test and Sheridan couldn't seem to settle down. Her stomach was twisted in knots and nothing Fatima brought seemed appealing. She finally tried a little bread and some sparkling water and settled onto the couch to read for a bit when the door to her suite opened and Rashid walked in without preamble.

Emotion flooded her in an instant: happiness, anger, fear, sorrow. So many things it was hard to sort them all out, and all caused by this dark man who stood there in a smartly tailored gray suit and Kyrian headdress. Not for the first time, he made her heart skip a beat.

"Fatima says you aren't eating," he said, his voice tight and diamond edged. Just the way she expected it.

Of course he was getting reports about her. "I'm not hungry."

He came over and glared down at her. If he would put his hands on his hips, it would be the perfect admonishing parent pose.

"You have to eat. It's not good for you or the baby not to eat."

She put her hand over her belly automatically. “We don’t know if there is a baby.”

“We will know soon enough. Besides, it’s better to assume there is a baby and do everything to take care of it properly.”

She wanted to yell at him. “I didn’t refuse, Rashid. I can’t keep anything down right now. My stomach is upset.” She set the book aside and matched his glare. “You promised we would spend some time together so we could know each other better, and yet I’ve not seen you in five days now.”

His expression didn’t ease. “I’ve been busy. This is what happens when one is a king.”

“Yet you found time to come here tonight and chastise me for not eating.”

He stripped off the *kaffiyeh* and tossed it aside. Then he raked a hand through his hair. “I came straight here from a meeting.” He walked over to the table where Fatima had left food in chafing dishes and examined the contents. Then he picked up a plate and dished some things onto it.

Sheridan bristled. “If you think you’re going to force me to eat—”

“Not at all,” he said, picking up a fork and heading over to sit in a nearby chair. “I haven’t eaten yet and I’m starving.”

Sheridan blinked. After days of silence, he was planning to eat with her? He’d taken her to bed, made her feel things that excited and confused her and then when she’d been certain he was planning to do it again, he’d left her standing alone in the courtyard.

To say she didn’t understand him was an understatement.

"Wow, I'm being graced with your majestic presence for dinner? I'm honored."

He looked up at her, his eyes gleaming. But not with anger. "You said you wanted to talk to me. Here I am. Talk. Bore me silly if you must."

She folded her arms. "Perhaps I'm a sparkling conversationalist. Did you ever consider that?"

"It has not been my experience with most women, but perhaps you will be different."

She told herself it would be unwise to throw a pillow at him. She chose instead to focus on one aspect of what he'd said. "Most women? Who has managed to please you conversationally?"

He took a bite of food, chewed and swallowed. She didn't think he would answer her, but then he looked up again and speared her with his hot gaze. "My wife did," he said. "Not always, it's true. But often enough. She died five years ago, in case you were wondering."

Her belly had tightened into a hot ball of nerves. Of all the things he could have said, she hadn't seen that one coming. Her heart ached for him. "I'm sorry, Rashid."

She didn't know what else to say. To lose someone you loved had to be such a tragedy. And someone so young, too. No wonder he sometimes seemed cold and lonely. It made sense now.

He set the plate aside. "This is not something I speak of, but if we are to marry, I thought you should know it."

Her throat was tight and her heart hammered in her stomach, her chest, her ears. "I appreciate you telling me. But I'm not certain marriage is the answer to our dilemma. Assuming there is one."

He frowned. "This child has to be born legitimate, Sheridan. It is the only way."

Panic bloomed inside her. She didn't want to take away a child's heritage, but she also didn't want to have to marry a man she hardly knew. They had sexual chemistry, but what if that was all they had? How could she live a lifetime with a man who'd only married her to claim a child?

"I assume I have no say in this?"

"You would prefer options? Marry me and be this child's mother, or go home after you give birth. Those are your options."

She figured it was a good thing there were no weapons nearby. "Those aren't options."

His eyes flashed. "They are the ones you have."

"I won't leave my child."

"No, I didn't think you would. I might have thought so once, but no longer."

Her head was beginning to ache. "And what brought about this blinding revelation?"

"Daoud tells me you've been playing with the puppies. Feeding them, taking care of them. And then there is my kitchen staff, Fatima and even the stable hands. They like you, and you like them. They all say how kind you are, how caring. Yet even without these things, there is this deed you set out to do for your sister. You are a giving person, Sheridan, but I don't believe you are so giving as to leave your child in Kyr. You will stay."

His words wrapped around her heart and squeezed. She liked Daoud, Fatima and the kitchen staff. To know they liked her, too, was touching. "There is every possibility I will go home tomorrow."

"Yes, there is."

Pain sliced into her at the thought. It confused her. She wanted to go home, wanted to go back to her life in Savannah, her business, her friends. She wanted her life the way it was before Rashid al-Hassan had walked into it.

And yet that thought filled her with despair. Never to see him again? Never to make love to him? He didn't seem much bothered either way, and that hurt, too.

"All this talk of marriage is premature," she said tightly.

"Is it? We will know tomorrow. If you are pregnant, things must be done quickly."

"And you've already decided everything. Without asking me what I might want."

It was just like him, of course. King Rashid acted. He did not consult a soul. He simply did what he deemed best. Just like when he'd scooped her up and brought her to Kyr against her will.

"I have told you your options." His voice was smooth and even, as if he was explaining things to a child.

Anger wrapped long fingers around her throat and squeezed. "I still have Annie to consider. What about her?"

His expression grew hard. Hard and cold and unapproachable. "What about her?"

That was the moment when the bile in Sheridan's stomach started swirling hard, pushing upward, demanding release. She got to her feet and staggered toward the bathroom. She barely made it in time, and then she was bending over the sink, retching.

There was a hand in her hair, holding it back. He put another hand on her back and rubbed gently while tears sprang to her eyes and she felt utterly miserable. She wanted to tell him to stop touching her, but in fact it felt nice to have him soothe her. She was a traitor even to herself.

"I'm not trying to be harsh," he said, his voice gentle for once. "But your sister cannot figure into my dynastic responsibilities. There are other solutions to her problem. You told me yourself about an experimental treatment."

Sheridan put her hands on the counter, bracing herself, her eyes squeezed shut as she prayed there was nothing else left to come up.

"They can't afford it," she said miserably when she could speak.

"I can."

Sheridan turned on the water and gulped some down before she straightened shakily and turned to face him. His beauty always hit her with a punch and now was no exception. A king had just held her hair while she'd thrown up the little bit of food she'd managed to eat.

If anyone had ever told her such a thing could happen, she'd have never believed them.

"You would do that for them?" Her heart was still pounding, but for a different reason now. It was everything she could have wanted for Annie. There were no guarantees the treatment would work, but it was a chance.

"I would not do it for them," Rashid said very softly. "I would do it for you."

Rashid watched her mouth fall open on a soft "oh" and was seized with a desire to claim her lips and take everything he desired. But she wasn't feeling well, and he hadn't come here for that anyway.

No, he'd come because Fatima had said she wasn't eating. And because he'd been getting endless reports about her roaming the palace, commenting on the architecture, talking with endless people, playing with orphaned puppies and spending time in the kitchen discussing recipes and food service.

At a recent lunch he'd attended with some visiting dignitaries, the napkins were folded in shapes. They had been lotus flowers, he'd realized, and he'd been so fascinated that he'd missed the first half of what one of the dignitaries had been saying to him about water rights and oil production.

When he'd asked about it afterward, someone had told him that Miss Sloane had taught the staff how to do it. Lotus napkins. Puppies. Even Daoud spoke her name with a quiet reverence that set Rashid's teeth on edge.

Everyone liked Miss Sloane, and that had made him think about her more than he wished. He liked her, too, but in a different way. He liked the way her body moved beneath his, the sounds she made when she came and the way her mouth tasted his so greedily. He'd thought about it for days now.

He'd deliberately stayed away because he didn't trust himself not to act upon the hot feelings she ignited in him.

He'd been right, considering that he was staring at her mouth and thinking about it drifting over his skin.

Her eyes filled with tears. It was almost a shock, considering that she'd been so strong from the moment he'd first seen her until now. One spilled down her cheek and she quickly dashed it away.

"I don't know what to say." She pulled in a breath and rubbed her hand over her mouth.

His throat was tight and he didn't know why. He cleared it. "You need to rest, *habibti*."

She pushed a lock of golden hair behind her ear. Her fingers were trembling. "Yes, I probably should. I am quite tired."

She was sagging against the counter and he reached over and swept her into his arms.

"What are you doing?" she gasped.

She was so light, so small. She weighed nothing and it made something move deep in his chest as he thought of her huge with child. "Taking you to bed."

Her cheeks reddened. "I don't feel up to, to..."

He carried her into the bedroom and set her on the bed. "And that is not what I'm suggesting."

He picked up her gown from where it lay neatly folded on her pillow and handed it to her. She clutched it to her chest. On impulse, he ran his fingers over her cheek.

"Change. I'm going to finish eating. Then I will come back. If you still wish to talk, we will talk."

Her eyes were red rimmed. "All right."

He turned away and went back into the living area to finish eating while she changed. He didn't like the way she'd seemed so shattered just now. So stunned and confused. He preferred the Sheridan who stood up to him. The Sheridan who got spitting mad and told him there was no way she would give up her baby.

That Sheridan was strong and would survive anything he threw at her. Anything the world threw at her. But would she survive a baby? She was so small, so delicate.

Rashid couldn't help the memories crowding his head. They made him shiver, made him ache. He would not go through that again. His heart had to remain hard, no matter that Sheridan threatened to soften it.

When he figured she'd had enough time to change, he strode back toward her room, expecting her to pelt him with questions or rebuke him for making decisions for her. Perhaps he'd let her say whatever she wished, since her fire aroused him, and then maybe he'd undress and climb in bed with her. If one thing led to another, who was he to complain?

But when he got there, she was sound asleep in the middle of the bed.

CHAPTER NINE

"THE TEST IS POSITIVE."

The doctor, a lean, short man with glasses, was looking at the results on a printout. No peeing on a stick for Sheridan. It had been far more involved, with urine and blood samples and an excruciating wait while the lab processed the results. "Your hCG levels are doubling nicely and all looks normal at this stage."

Sheridan sat in her chair in Rashid's office and felt as if her heart had stopped. Across from her, Rashid sat at his desk, his lips compressed into a tight line. The doctor seemed oblivious to the undercurrents in the room as he stood and bowed low.

"Congratulations, Your Majesty."

Rashid waved the man out and then they were alone. But Rashid didn't speak. He simply sat there with that bloodless look on his face until her belly was a tight ball of nerves.

"I'm not sure I really believed it would happen the first time." Her voice shook but Rashid didn't seem to notice.

He looked up at her as if just realizing she was there. "What?"

But he didn't wait for an answer. He sprang to his

feet and began pacing like a caged beast. He was wearing his desert robes today, complete with the headdress held in place by a golden *igal.* He was regal and magnificent and breathtaking. She watched him pacing, her hand over her stomach, and tried to come to grips with the fact she was having his baby.

"We'll marry immediately. The council will have to be informed and then we can sign the documents. We can have a wedding ceremony for the public, but that can be done in a few weeks. You won't be showing by then and—"

"Stop." Sheridan was on her feet, her blood pounding in her throat and temples. She didn't know why she'd spoken, but she felt as if her entire life was altering right before her eyes and there was nothing she could do to stop the tidal wave of change.

Rashid was looking at her now, his dark gaze dangerous and compelling. She reminded herself that he was capable of tenderness. He had touched her tenderly only last night when holding her hair and rubbing her back. And then there was the night he'd made love to her, so hot and intense and, yes, tender in his own way.

"You're making all these plans without asking me how I feel about any of them."

His brows drew down. "This is the way things are done in Kyr. How would you know what the arrangements should be?"

She dug her fingernails into her palms. She was sweating, but not from illness. From shock. And fear.

"I wasn't talking about how things are done in Kyr. I'm talking about this marriage."

As if she could refuse it. She was here, in his palace, and he was a king. This child had to be born legitimate.

And he'd said he would pay for Annie's treatment. What more could she want?

Love. Yes, she could want love. She could want to marry a man because she loved him, not because she had to.

His gaze narrowed. "You are pregnant—this marriage will take place."

She held her arms stiffly at her sides. "Maybe I want to be asked. Did you ever consider that? Maybe I wanted to get married in an old church somewhere, with my family surrounding me, and maybe I wanted to be in love with the man I marry."

Oh, why say that out loud? Why let him know what a hopeless romantic you are?

His expression grew hard. "Life does not always give us what we want. We have to take what's offered and do the best we can with it."

Her heart fell. He was infuriating. Cold and calculating and arrogant. She wanted him to care, at least a little bit, about what this meant for her. To him, she was a woman who carried a potential king. He wanted to order her about the way he ordered Daoud or Fatima or Mostafa.

And she knew, if she knew nothing else, that she couldn't allow him to do that without protest.

"I didn't say yes yet. You're making plans and I didn't say yes."

There was a huge lump in her throat now. Huge. It was like she'd swallowed all the pain she'd ever felt and was about to choke on it.

He picked up a pen on his desk and flipped it in his fingers as if he needed something to do. As if he was irritated. "You are carrying my child and we are going to marry. There's nothing to say yes to." He fixed her with a hard stare. "But if you could say no, would you? Knowing what's at stake for everyone involved, would you say no and deny your child the opportunity to be my heir? Or your sister the chance to have her own child?"

Sheridan's throat hurt. "I didn't say that."

He threw the pen down and sank into his chair again. "Then I fail to see the problem. You will be a princess consort, *habibti.* You will have a life of privilege. And you will be the mother of our child, which is what you've assured me you want. Or am I mistaken? Would you rather leave the child with me and return to America once he is born?"

Sheridan clenched her fists in her lap. Once more, it was a good thing there were no weapons handy. "This baby might be a girl, you know. And no, I don't want to leave her with you."

"Then we will marry immediately and be done with this matter."

This matter. As if marriage and children were the equivalent of deciding where to go on vacation or which carpet to order for the new house.

"Thank you for settling that." Sheridan got to her feet. She was shaking with rage and fear, and sick with the helplessness she felt. "I guess I'll return to my rooms now and await your next command. How I got through life for twenty-six years without you to tell me what to do is quite the mystery. I'm pleased I don't have to think for myself a moment longer."

"Careful, Sheridan," he growled.

A sensual shiver traveled down her spine at the sound. Oh, what was it about him growling at her that turned her on? She'd just told him off for being autocratic, so why did part of her thrill at the edge in his voice?

"Why? If I make a mistake, you'll just tell me what to do to correct it." She sank into the deepest curtsy she'd yet done and then turned and strode toward the door. He was there before her, his arm shooting out and wrapping around her before she could escape.

Her breath caught as he spun her around. "You dare to walk out on a king?"

"You aren't *my* king," she said hotly. But her body was melting where it touched his and that inconvenient fire was beginning to sizzle through her.

"Maybe I am," he said, his voice heavy and angry at once. "Maybe I am utterly *your* king."

Her reply was lost as he ripped the hijab from her hair. "You're mine now, Sheridan," he said hotly, backing her against the wall and pressing his body to hers. "And I keep what's mine."

And then he brought his mouth down on hers. Sheridan stiffened. She was determined to fight him, to keep her mouth closed to his invasion, to push him away.

But she did none of those things. Of course she didn't. Rashid al-Hassan was an unstoppable sensual force and he had a power over her that she couldn't deny. His tongue slid between her lips, demanding her response—and then they were kissing each other frantically, hotly, with all the pent-up passion of the past few days of deprivation. She'd never had such a physical connection to a man before. A connection that went against sense and reason and just *was*.

His hands spanned her rib cage, his thumbs grazing her nipples as he pinned her body to the wall with his own. Her pulse raced as her nipples tightened painfully. Her breasts were so sensitive now and they both knew why.

He found the closures to her dress and opened them deftly. Then he was pushing the garment off her shoulders, letting it fall to the floor. She wrapped her arms around his neck and arched into him until he growled again and stepped back to rip her panties down her legs. She stepped out of them as she fumbled with the soft trousers he wore beneath his *dishdasha,* trying to free him.

He helped her and soon she had her hands on his hot erection. But he didn't give her a chance to play. His broad hands went to her bottom, lifted her high against the wall—and then he plunged into her as they both gasped.

"Sheridan." His voice was a hot whisper in her ear and her heart twisted tight. "I need you."

"Kiss me, Rashid," she begged. Her skin was too tight, her belly too hollow, her body too hot. She needed the things he gave her, needed the connection and release. She didn't understand it, but she craved it. Craved him.

He fused his mouth to hers—and then he began to drive up into her, harder and faster and deeper than before, until her body was alive with sensation, until she had to wrench her mouth from his and sob his name as she splintered apart in his arms.

He didn't release her, though. He took her again and again, until she was a quivering mass of nerve endings, until her body couldn't take another moment's pleasure, until he finally let go of his rigid control and came, his seed filling her in warm jets.

He laid his forehead against the wall behind her, his

breath coming in gusts. His skin was hot and moist and so was hers. She turned her head into him, tasted the salt on his skin on impulse.

And found herself released. He stepped away from her and fixed his trousers, then reached down and picked up her gown for her. She snatched it out of his hand and he met her gaze evenly.

They stared at each other for a long moment, her clutching the dress in front of her like a shield, him clenching his fingers into tight fists at his side. As if he wanted to touch her again but had to force himself not to.

Her legs were weak and anger bubbled hot in her veins, but if he reached for her, if he kissed her again, she'd open to him like a flower.

And she really despised that about herself. There was such a thing as being delightfully impulsive, as being friendly and open, but this was too much.

"I don't understand you," she said. "If you don't like being with me, why do you touch me in the first place?"

She thought they had a chemistry that was unusual, but maybe she was fooling herself. Maybe he just saw her as an option for quick sex. He found his pleasure in her body and he was done. And she was just stupid enough to make the same mistake twice.

He shoved a hand through his hair. "I like being with you. But it's over and I have work to do."

She shook out her dress angrily and slipped into it. Then she turned her back on him. "I can't do this without your help."

He came over and stood behind her, his fingers brushing her skin as he zipped her up and fastened the hooks. When he finished, she turned around and glared at him.

"This can't happen again," she told him tightly. "I

have feelings, Rashid, and I won't let you stomp all over them just to get your way. And another thing," she added, pointing at him. "There are women in this palace in dresses and business suits and slacks. I've seen them, and while I played along with your commands to dress as a Kyrian woman, I won't blindly do it anymore. Kyrian women seem to represent a range of styles, which you purposely did not tell me. If I want to wear my jeans, I'm wearing them."

His expression was tightly controlled. "When you appear before the council, you will wear traditional clothing. Aside from that, I don't care."

She lifted her chin as she met his dark stare. "Oh, I already gathered that, Rashid. You don't care at all."

Rashid met with the council and informed them he would be marrying, and why. The council wasn't pleased that Sheridan wasn't Kyrian, but they could hardly argue with the fact she was carrying his child.

"And would you consider a Kyrian woman for a second wife, Your Majesty?" one of the men asked.

Rashid let his hard stare glide over the gathering. They were good men, wise men, men whose families had spent generations on the council. And while they had gotten far more progressive over the years, they still clung to some traditions. A pure Kyrian dynasty was one of those, though they all knew that past sheikhs had sometimes married foreigners and had children with them. Still, it cost him nothing to appease them. They would not accept Sheridan as queen, but as a princess consort. And with a future queen of Kyrian descent to be named, they would be happy.

"I will," he said coolly. "But not immediately."

That seemed to satisfy them and the council was dismissed. Rashid returned to his office to work, but he couldn't seem to stop picturing Sheridan up against the wall, her lovely legs wrapped around him, her sweet voice panting in his ear as he took her over the edge.

He pushed back from his desk and sat there staring at the place where they'd been. He'd taken her like a savage. Like a man for whom control was impossible to attain, when nothing could be further from the truth.

She wound him into knots and he didn't like it. She'd said he didn't care, but he very much feared he might. Not a lot, certainly, but more than he was comfortable with. Because he couldn't stop thinking about her, or about how it felt to lose himself in her body.

He was not the sort of man to become obsessed with a woman, yet she intrigued him. Had from the first moment he'd seen her standing in her shop, all small and blond and seemingly sweet.

But then he'd kissed her and his world had gone sideways. He'd wanted her every moment since.

And he hated that he did.

She was pregnant. Thinking the words sent that same cold chill through him, as always—but there was something else, too. Pride, possession, ownership. She was carrying his child and he was going to marry her. For Kyr.

Rashid got to his feet and left the office, striding through the palace until he came to his rooms. It wasn't quite dark yet, but the hour was growing late. He changed into jeans—not without thinking of her informing him that she would be wearing her jeans whenever she wanted, that defiant tilt to her chin—and a button-down shirt, and then went through his suite of rooms to the hidden door that connected to the women's quarters.

He stood there for a long moment, staring at the lock. And then he released it and stepped inside. She wasn't in bed so he moved through the rooms until he saw her at the computer. She was hunched over it, her head in her hands, and his heart squeezed.

Then she reached for a tissue and he knew she was crying. Damn it. His fault, no doubt. Because he'd pushed her away. But how could he explain to her that being in her arms after they had sex felt like a betrayal? Not because of the sex, but because of the way he wanted to linger, the way he wanted to know everything about her.

"Sheridan."

She startled, shooting up out of her chair and whirling to face him. Her nose was red. "My God, you scared me to death."

"I'm sorry."

She was wearing her jeans and a silky shirt and she looked so small and alone as she stood there with her shoulders bent. "How did you get in here?"

"There's a hidden door in the bedroom. It leads to my rooms."

"Oh," she said softly, and he knew she must be wondering why he hadn't used it to bring her back the other night. But there were more immediate things to think about.

"What is wrong?"

She gave a half shrug. "I was just reading email from my business partner. I think we're both realizing our dream is over now."

"I know you blame me for these things, but I am not

the one who caused this." And yet he did feel guilty for his part in changing her life.

"Believe it or not, I do know that. But it seems so odd that a single oversight could impact so many lives."

"This is quite often the case."

"For a king, I'm sure it is. For a girl from Savannah who just wanted to give her sister a gift, this is all a bit of a shock."

She walked over and put her hands on the back of a chair, gripping it so tightly that her knuckles whitened. He watched her, torn between going to her and holding her and staying where he was. In the end, he decided to stay. She would not welcome him at the moment.

She swiped the tissue over her nose again and stuffed it in her pocket. "So what did you come here to tell me to do now?"

Rashid's brows drew down. Why had he come? *Because you can't stay away. Because she has a brightness to her that draws you like a moth. Because you want to feel that brightness wrapped around you again.*

"I didn't come to tell you to do anything."

She waved a hand as if she were sweeping aside a bothersome fly. "Well, isn't that a relief? What can I help you with, then?"

For once in his life, he was left with nothing to say. He dug down into the recesses of his brain. "My brother is going to build a skyscraper for me. I understand you have architecture experience. Perhaps you could consult?"

She blinked at him. Several times. "I…well, I did train as an architect, but I worked on historical preservation. Old buildings. Skyscrapers aren't quite my thing. Not to mention I left the profession to start Dixie Doin's with Kelly."

"Why did you do that?" He truly wanted to know. She'd gone to school for one thing and ended up doing another.

She shrugged. "I enjoyed architecture, but it wasn't as fun as party planning. I like organizing things, making people happy. Preserving old buildings takes time, but making people happy with food and fun is instant gratification."

"Which explains why you spend so much time in the kitchen. I enjoyed the lotus-shaped napkins, by the way."

She smiled at him, a genuine smile for once, and his heart did that little hitch thing again. "I'm glad. I'll show them ferns next. Then maybe some swans."

"No swans at the state dinner, I beg you."

She laughed. "Fine, no swans." But then her smile faded and she slumped against the back of the chair. "Will I get to attend these functions, or am I to be kept shut away like that cousin you can't trust not to drink too much and dance on the tables?"

The way she said things amused him. "Do you drink too much or dance on tables?"

"Not since college." He must have looked surprised because she laughed again. "I'm kidding. I danced on the tables *without* drinking. Because it was fun sometimes to let loose."

He tried to imagine her on top of a table, dancing and having fun. "Do you let loose often?"

She hesitated a moment. "Too often where you're concerned."

The words hung in the air between them. He could feel his body hardening, and she hadn't said anything provocative. Or done anything provocative. But he knew how she tasted, how she felt, and he wanted to unwrap her and taste and feel her again.

And again.

"We've only been together twice," he pointed out.

"And if you hadn't avoided me for so long, I imagine it would have been far more often than that. Though I suppose it's a very good thing you did."

Okay, he was seriously hard now. Ready to walk over there and take her in his arms. "You say the most unexpected things."

"I'm too honest for my own good sometimes. I've always been this way, but I like it because it beats keeping things inside."

"But you do keep some things inside." He was thinking of her sister and the way she defended the other woman's weaknesses even when they affected her life. He wondered why she did that, but he supposed he didn't really have to ask. When he'd been a kid, he'd done everything he could to keep Kadir insulated from their father's wrath. It hadn't always worked, but he'd tried.

She bowed her head. "I suppose I do. But everyone needs a few secrets, right?"

Who was he to contradict her? He had secrets of his own. "I don't know if *needs* is the right word. But yes, I know what you mean."

Her blue eyes gleamed. "I'm still angry with you. But if you walked over here and took me in your arms, you could make me forget it all for a few hours."

He was poised to do just that when she continued.

"But I'm asking you not to." She shook her head. "I need time to process this, Rashid. I need time to figure out how to fit my life into this box you've handed me. I can't do that if you confuse me with sex."

CHAPTER TEN

SHERIDAN'S HEART POUNDED as she gazed at the handsome sheikh standing across the room. Just a word from her and he would cross the distance separating them and make her feel as if she were the most important, wonderful thing in his life for a few hours.

But she couldn't let it happen again. Not after the way she'd felt this afternoon when they'd made love so urgently against a wall. After, when she'd felt shattered by the emotions he stirred inside her, when she'd needed tenderness and closeness, he'd pushed her away. Every effort she made to be close to him, he rebuffed. So why did she keep doing it?

And now she had to marry him. She didn't know how she was going to survive if she had to keep navigating a sexual minefield with him. They'd done everything backward. Baby, sex and now marriage, and she couldn't keep going down the same path without knowing who he was. Really knowing.

"The sex doesn't mean anything to you," she said. He did not contradict her, and her belly squeezed a little tighter. "And it doesn't mean anything to me either, but it could start to mean more than it should just because I feel so out of place here."

That was what truly frightened her. She was a stranger in a strange land, wholly dependent on this man, bound to him by ties greater than any devised by law. She had to keep her feelings grounded in reality. To do that, she couldn't fall into bed with him every time he came near her.

He shoved his hands into his pockets—God, he was delicious in faded jeans—and adopted a casual pose that belied the tension in the set of his shoulders. He was a man poised on the edge of action. Always. That he would attempt to hide that from her was encouraging.

Because they both knew who had the true power. That he would allow her to have her own both stunned and warmed her. It was progress.

"I am not trying to place you in a box. You seem not to realize how very privileged your life is about to become."

"A gilded box is still a box."

He rubbed a temple and came around to sink down on the cushions of a settee. "I do in fact know this." He leaned back and gazed up at the domed ceiling above them. "I hated living in this palace as a child. It was hell in many ways."

She came around the chair and perched on the edge of it, her heart in her throat and a dull pain stinging her eyes.

He shrugged. "My father was a harsh man, *habibti*. He did not believe in sparing the rod, so to speak."

She swallowed. Was he actually sharing things with her? Or was this an anomaly? "I heard that you only recently returned to Kyr. Is that why?"

His eyes glittered. "The palace is full of information, it would seem."

"The person I heard it from seemed rather terrified to impart it. As if you would be angry. As if you are a tyrant who punishes people for slights."

He looked rather stunned at that revelation. "I am a king, and I must be harsh at times. But I am not a tyrant. The only people who feel my wrath are the council and my immediate staff. I have no need to terrify maids or cooks, I assure you."

"Honestly, I didn't think you did." Because the people she'd met seemed happy to have him as their king, though they were also more than a little awestruck by him. He didn't speak much, they said. He kept to himself. He was serious and responsible and he didn't smile.

But he was fair. No one had yet claimed he wasn't.

One dark eyebrow arched as if he didn't quite believe her. "Really? I would imagine you were my greatest critic. Did I not kidnap you and force you to come to Kyr? Am I not forcing you to marry me against your will?"

She clasped her hands together in her lap. "Well, those things are pretty bad and you should feel quite ashamed of yourself. But you haven't been cruel. Exasperating and arrogant, but never cruel."

He held her gaze steadily. "I am intimately acquainted with cruelty, and therefore I have striven never to be the kind of man who resorts to it in order to achieve his aims."

Again, her heart twisted for the child he'd been. "I believe you."

He blew out a breath. "Well, we have progress, then." He stood suddenly. "Good night, Sheridan. Sleep well."

"Rashid, wait."

He turned back to her, a question in his expression.

Why had she stopped him? What did she want to say? Her heart beat hard and her throat ached and she didn't understand this urge to go to him and wrap her arms around him. Not for the sexual chemistry, but for the boy he'd once been. The boy who'd had a cruel father and hadn't known much love.

She wanted to know more. So much more. But he was finished and she didn't know how to make him start again.

"Sleep well," she said, her voice little more than a whisper.

He tilted his head in acknowledgment. And then he was gone.

Kadir al-Hassan arrived the next day with his wife, Emily. Sheridan had just returned from playing with the puppies when she found the palace staff in an uproar. Or the domestic staff anyway. She swallowed hard and hurried to her room to change out of her jeans and T-shirt. It was quite a relief to be able to dress in something she wasn't worried about getting dirty, though she'd chosen to wear the hijab, too. She liked the fabric covering her head when she went out into the hot Kyrian sunshine. It helped keep her cool.

Now she hesitated as she stood in her closet. She had her clothes from home and the Kyrian clothing. In the end, she chose to wear a blouse and trousers with the hijab. Then she checked her email and waited nervously for someone to decide she should be sent for.

Finally, there was a knock at her door and Emily al-Hassan was on the other side. She was a pretty girl, tall and slender and elegantly dressed in a designer suit and low heels. And she was smiling.

"You must be Sheridan," she said after she introduced herself. "I'm so pleased to meet you."

Sheridan was happy to meet her, too. Emily was American, and it was like having a visitor from home even though they'd never met before.

Emily took a seat and talked easily while Fatima arrived with tea. Once Fatima was gone, Emily's expression changed to something more sympathetic and concerned.

"How are you holding up?" she asked. "Is Rashid behaving himself?"

Sheridan felt a little odd talking about her life with a stranger, but then Emily was the only other person she knew who shared the novel experience of marrying a Kyrian royal.

"I'm not sure he knows how," Sheridan said, and Emily laughed.

"Truthfully, when I first met him, Rashid scared me half to death. He's so quiet. So intense." She frowned then. "I probably shouldn't say anything, but you are marrying him now and so I feel you should be armed with as much information as possible. Rashid and Kadir didn't have a good relationship with their father. He was very harsh."

"Rashid mentioned it."

Emily's eyes widened a bit. "Did he? How interesting. Did he also mention that their father refused to choose an heir? It should have always been Rashid, but King Zaid wanted to punish him. So he left the succession undecided."

"But he decided in the end."

Emily sipped her tea. "No. Kadir did. Rashid did not come when their father died, and so Kadir had to take the throne. But Rashid finally showed up before the formal declaration. And Kadir abdicated."

Sheridan blinked. "Why would he do that?"

Emily's cheeks reddened a bit then. "It's a long story, but he did it for me. I was too scandalous for Kyr, you see. And Kadir never wanted to be a king. He only married me to get out of it."

"But you're still married."

Emily laughed. "Oh, yes. Marrying Kadir for all the wrong reasons is still the best thing I ever did. Because it turns out the reasons were right in the end."

Sheridan's throat ached. It was clear that Emily al-Hassan loved her husband very much. And he must love her equally as much to have given up a throne. It was incredibly romantic. And it made her sad when she thought of her and Rashid and their impending marriage.

She shook her head as hot feelings welled up inside her. "I don't want to marry Rashid. I don't love him, and he doesn't love me. But there's the baby to consider. A baby born to an unmarried mother can't inherit a throne, apparently, even when the king of Kyr is most definitely the father. And forget shared custody." She waved a hand. "Not happening here."

"No, that is definitely Kyr for you." Emily leaned forward and squeezed her hand. Sheridan liked how sympathetic and friendly the other woman was. "Kyr has its charms, and the al-Hassan brothers have even more. I promise you they are worth it in the end. Even grouchy Rashid."

Sheridan laughed. She'd been on the edge of tears, but laughing helped to banish them. At least temporarily. God, she'd needed this. Someone who didn't think the sun rose and set on Rashid, who knew he was flawed and who didn't mind saying it.

"He is grouchy," she said. "And bossy."

Emily laughed. "Bossiness is an al-Hassan trait. But you have to admit they are devilishly handsome."

"I haven't seen your husband yet, but if he looks anything like Rashid, I'd say you're a very lucky woman."

Emily's eyebrows waggled. "I am a *very* lucky woman. And you will be, too, once you tame Rashid."

Sheridan sighed. The other woman was so certain everything would work out in the end. Sheridan didn't feel that way at all. She thought of Rashid pushing her away after sex and her heart wanted to break. "I don't know that he's tamable. Or that I want to. In truth, I wish I could just go home."

But that wasn't as true as she claimed, and she felt a blush stain her cheeks. Emily very politely didn't comment.

"Would you like more tea?" Emily asked instead, reaching for the pot.

"Please."

After they settled down with fresh cups, Emily looked at her very thoughtfully. "Kadir tells me that Rashid has always been intense, but he has not always been the sort of emotionally closed-off man he is now. Kadir does not know what happened, but he thinks something did. There were a few years when they only had the barest of contact. Kadir was building his business and Rashid was in Russia." Emily sipped her tea. "I've only known grouchy Rashid, so I can't say for certain. But Kadir loves his brother very much, and he would not do that if Rashid was not good."

Sheridan's heart thumped. She wouldn't have guessed

that Kadir didn't know about his brother's marriage and his wife's subsequent death, but clearly he did not. It wasn't her place to say anything, so she sipped her tea and kept silent. But she hurt for Rashid as she thought of him losing the woman he loved and having no one to turn to.

They sat there for another hour, chatting about many different things. Emily explained the Kyrian wedding procedure to Sheridan, who found it comfortingly sterile. Oh, she'd always wanted the big emotional wedding, but signing her name on a document and then watching Rashid do the same would be quite enough for her. It was like signing loan papers at the bank. She could handle that.

But when the time came to do just that later the same day, Sheridan found herself more emotional than she'd thought she would be. The signing took place in Rashid's office with Kadir and Emily for witnesses, along with the lawyers who presided over the entire thing. It lasted all of a few minutes as they sat on one side of a conference table with the lawyers on the other and Kadir and Emily at either end.

There was a translator who read the documents to Sheridan, and then she was directed to sign her name on a line. She could feel Rashid beside her, his gaze intent on her as if he expected her to refuse. She almost did. She almost stood and ran from the room, but in the end she knew it would merely be a stalling tactic.

She signed and put the pen down, then stared at her fingers clenched in her lap. Rashid scratched his signature across the document in a hasty scrawl, and then shoved the whole thing across the table.

He was angry, she realized, but she didn't know why.

She glanced over at Emily, who gave her a smile of encouragement and a firm nod, as if to say, "You can do this."

Another few moments and the men on the other side of the table were filing the documents into briefcases and rising. They left the room, and then Emily went to Kadir, who took her hand in his and gave her a look that could only be called hot. He was very handsome, of course. The al-Hassan brothers had been designed by God to make female hearts beat a little harder when they walked into a room.

"Congratulations, Rashid," Kadir said, shaking his brother's hand. "And Sheridan, welcome to the family."

He kissed her on both cheeks. Emily did the same while Kadir took his brother aside for a quick conversation at the other end of the room. Sheridan's heart was beating hard and her stomach fluttered.

"It'll be fine," Emily said. "He's a good man. He's just a little lost, I think. Kadir was, too, but we found our way." She squeezed Sheridan's shoulders. "You will, too. I'm certain of it."

Sheridan wished she shared Emily's confidence, but all she could do was smile wanly and thank the other woman for being there.

Kadir joined his wife then, his arm going around her shoulders. He couldn't seem to be near her without touching her. It made Sheridan wistful. Rashid touched her, but only to initiate sex. After he'd found his release, he was finished with the touching.

"We should leave them alone now, *habibti,*" Kadir said.

And then Kadir and Emily were gone and Sheridan was left standing in Rashid's private office—where they'd had mad sex against the wall—with the beautiful view of the sandstone cliffs in the distance on one side and the ocean on another. The room was quiet. Too quiet.

She turned to look at Rashid and found him watching her. He did not look pleased. She thought of him shoving the papers across the table and her belly tightened. He wanted to be married even less than she did, it would seem.

She thought of him last night, telling her about his wife. He'd said it plainly, unfeelingly, but she knew he must have been deeply affected by the death of the woman he'd loved.

And he must have loved her, since he'd married her willingly and not because she was pregnant with an heir to the throne.

Now he was married to her, and no matter how much he'd said it had to be done and there was no choice, he clearly wasn't happy about it now that it had taken place.

His frown deepened. "Kadir says you are frightened of me."

Sheridan shook her head. "I'm not."

"I didn't think you were. You've been giving me hell since the first moment I saw you. If you weren't frightened then, you could hardly be so now that I've made you a royal princess."

Her belly rolled with nerves. A princess, but not a queen. In order for there to be a queen, the king had to make a proclamation. That much she'd learned from Emily. And while it was silly to even think about the difference, it was quite obvious that Rashid did not intend to issue a proclamation. His father had never done so, either.

"I don't feel like a princess."

"You will soon enough. You'll have to go before the council, and then there are state functions to preside over, meetings to attend. You'll have a secretary and a staff. You will have to choose a cause to support, and then you will need to make appearances for it—"

"Rashid, please." He stopped speaking. There was no moisture in her throat at all. She thought of everything he'd just said and wanted to run and hide. She wasn't shy, but it was too much to process so soon. "Can I please get used to the idea of being married before you start throwing duties at me?"

He looked stiff. Formal. He was so incredibly handsome in his dark desert robes today. They were trimmed in fine gold embroidery that sparkled and shimmered as he moved. Her own dress—a deep purple silk gown with a cream hijab—was not as beautiful.

"Since you informed me you did not wish to be married, and that you did not like having nothing to do, I assumed you would be happy to do things that would take you away from me."

This conversation was like navigating a minefield. How did one respond? Did she ignore the jab about marriage and focus on the part about being busy? Or did she address them both?

"You know what my objections to this marriage are, so I'm not repeating them. And I *would* like to be busy, but the things you've mentioned are not like running a party-planning and catering business."

His mouth flattened. "Some of the skills are the same. You said you liked to make people happy. You will be doing the same as a royal princess. And there will be functions to plan, if you wish to be involved in that."

"I think you know I would."

"Then you will inform your secretary. She will arrange everything for you." He went over to his desk and shuffled through some papers while she stood there and felt like a kid who'd been called into the principal's office for misbehaving.

"Are you angry with me?" she finally asked, deciding that the only way to get anywhere with him was to speak her mind.

He looked up then, his dark gaze spearing her in place. Her blood thumped slowly in her veins at the heat she saw there.

"Angry? No."

He went back to what he was doing and she huffed a sigh. "Rashid, you don't act like someone who's not angry."

He dropped the papers he'd been going through and came around the desk. Then he leaned back on it and crossed his arms. "You looked like a lamb being dragged to the slaughter at that table just now."

Her blood was beginning to hum with irritation. It was a welcome feeling compared to the ones she'd been having. "You didn't seem all that happy, either. I don't think there was a person in this room who believed either of us wanted to get married, so don't you go blaming me for your mood."

"I do blame you, Sheridan. My mood is one of frustration. Because I could smell you beside me and I couldn't touch you. You've told me not to touch you and I won't. But it frustrates me greatly. A man should be able to touch his wife."

Her heart skipped. Of all the things she'd thought were bothering him…

The blood rushed wildly through her veins. He was

sexually frustrated, not angry. He wanted her. In spite of everything, little bubbles of excitement popped and fizzed in her tummy.

"I thought you said we would have a marriage in name only." Because he had said so in the car in Savannah, and though they'd already had sex twice, she wanted him to admit he'd changed his mind. Because she wasn't going to keep having wild encounters with him and then be sent away as if she'd somehow misbehaved.

His eyebrows shot up. "Do you honestly think after this past week that's going to happen?"

She shrugged. "You tell me. Both times we've been together, you couldn't wait to get away."

He put his forehead in one palm for a moment, his fingers spanning his temples. And then he was looking at her again.

"It's not you."

There was a pinch in her chest. "That's a cliché, Rashid. It's not you, it's me. It's also what people usually say right before they say something awful, like 'I think we need to take a break' or 'I just can't love you the way you deserve.'"

As soon as she said the word *love* she wished she could call it back. It had no place here, and judging by the way he was looking at her now, it never would.

"We are clearly not taking a break. We've only just started. And as for love…" His expression grew stony. "I'm not capable of it, Sheridan."

Sheridan swallowed hard. Why did it hurt to hear him say it? Did she really expect love to enter the equation?

Yes. Yes, she did. Maybe not now, but someday. How could you live with someone, have such undeniable sexual chemistry with them, and not fall in love at some point? It didn't seem possible. There was more heat between her and Rashid than there'd ever been in both of her other relationships combined.

But maybe that was just her. Maybe Rashid took that kind of response for granted.

Sheridan turned toward the door. "I think I should go now. You clearly have work to do."

"I'm not trying to hurt you, *habibti.*" She thought of the way Kadir had said that word to his wife and tears welled behind her eyes.

"Why would I be hurt?" She lifted her chin. "We are nothing to each other, Rashid. Apparently, we're going to remain that way."

CHAPTER ELEVEN

THEY ATE DINNER in Rashid's private dining room with Kadir and Emily. That was an exercise in torture for Sheridan since those two were so clearly in love that it hurt to watch. Not because she expected Rashid to love her or because she wanted to love him, but when you found yourself pregnant and married without a mention of love, you felt rather cheated over the whole thing.

Why had she used that word earlier? Because she'd been hurt, that was why, and she'd tried to cover it up. She'd blundered, and then she'd found herself stumbling down a path where her new husband had informed her that he wasn't capable of love. It was not an auspicious beginning to a marriage.

She'd half expected Rashid to stop her when she'd walked out on him earlier, but he'd not done so. When she'd walked out of his office, Daoud was there. And for the first time ever, he dropped to his knees and bowed his head.

"Your Royal Highness."

Sheridan had started to shake then. "Daoud, please. Get up."

He'd done so, his dark eyes searching her face in a way that warmed her. As if he'd been looking for sadness and willing to pummel whomever had made her so. But then he'd dropped his head again and she'd realized that Rashid was in the hall behind her.

"Take Her Highness to her room, Daoud. She needs to rest."

"Yes, Your Majesty."

So she'd rested. And when she'd finished resting, she'd gone to the stables to check on the puppies again. They were getting bigger by the day. Soon, Daoud informed her, they would be given to new homes and she wouldn't get to see them anymore. She'd picked one up and held its soft furry body against her cheek before handing it back to the groom and returning to the palace.

And now they were at dinner and Sheridan was trying to follow the conversation, though not doing a good job. They were speaking English, because Emily didn't speak Arabic either, but the laughter and sound of voices just droned over her head while she wallowed in her own misery over her situation.

She'd spoken to Annie earlier, and Chris. Annie was over the moon with excitement about seeing the specialist. Chris was more subdued, as if he knew what this opportunity was costing Sheridan. But he was grateful nevertheless. He expressed it adequately enough for them both, though Sheridan might have liked her sister to realize how huge a change was occurring in her life.

For Annie, the prize was a baby of her own. Nothing and no one got in the way of that fact.

Kelly had been shocked, but she'd taken it all in and started making plans for the future of Dixie Doin's without Sheridan. That had hurt, but it was also necessary.

"Sheridan. Sheridan?"

She stirred after her name was repeated and looked up to find three sets of eyes looking back at her.

"Are you ill?" Rashid asked. "Do you need to lie down?"

She shook her head. "No, I'm fine. I was just thinking." She smiled as she picked up her water glass. "Please don't stop talking on my account."

Kadir shot his wife a look. "Actually, we were going to turn in. It's been a long day."

"Yes," Emily said. "I'm pretty tired. It's been a lovely day, though."

Everyone agreed it had been a lovely day. And then they took their leave of each other with hugs and kisses on the cheek. The room was quiet when Kadir and Emily were gone. Oppressively so, just like before.

"We keep finding ourselves alone together in spite of our best efforts," Sheridan said cheerfully as she turned toward Rashid.

"This is not necessarily a bad thing." Rashid's gaze was bright. Hot. And her stomach flipped even as her body began to melt at the promise in those eyes.

"I think I should go."

"And what if I said your place tonight is here? In my bed?"

She felt light-headed, dizzy. It was anticipation, fear and, yes, even a certain kind of joy she found astonishing.

"I don't think that's wise," she said, even though the voice in her head said something else entirely.

He moved toward her, took her hand and slowly pulled her into his arms. She went reluctantly, but she went. Her palms rested on his broad chest as his heat slid into her bones, her blood. Why did being held by

Rashid feel so right? And why did she want to wrap her arms around him and comfort him? She wanted to know why he had that haunted look in his eyes, and she wanted to know why he pushed her away in the most tender of moments.

"I think it's very wise," he told her. "The wisest thing possible."

His head dipped toward hers and her eyes drifted closed. But then she pictured how it would go. The delicious silkiness of his kiss, the inflammatory response of her own, the frantic revealing of bodies and the cataclysmic joining that would strip all her defenses and leave her heart bare.

And then the ice at the end. She couldn't take the ice.

"I'd rather talk," she blurted out.

He stopped, his lips a whisper away from hers. "Sheridan, you torture me."

Her fingers curled into his shirt. "We can't keep having wild sex like this, Rashid. We have to talk sometime."

He straightened, looking perfectly dejected. Like a kid who'd just had a treat taken away. "I don't see why we can't have sex first and then talk."

"Because you won't talk then. You'll run, or you'll take me back to my rooms, and nothing will ever get said."

He studied her very solemnly. And then he stepped back and drew her into the living area. She sank onto one of the couches and curled her feet beneath her. Rashid went to the opposite end of the couch.

"What do you wish to talk about?"

Sheridan bit her lip as she watched him. What did she wish to talk about? Anything. Everything. Only she'd never really expected he would do as she asked, so here she was with no leading question. No carefully thought-out phrase to begin prying into his life.

So she launched into it like a cannonball off a diving board.

"Why are you incapable of love?"

His eyes widened. And then his mouth flattened and she was certain he would brush her off. He did not, however, but she found herself almost wishing he had.

"Because it hurts. Because people die and you're left figuring out how to live your life without them. It's easier not to love."

"But choosing not to love and being incapable of it are two different things, right?"

He rubbed a hand over his face and looked away from her. "Maybe so. But I've chosen what works best for me."

"You will love this child, though." She wanted to understand him. He'd lost a wife and that had affected him greatly. But surely he would love their baby. She needed to know he was capable of that much at least.

"Sheridan." He didn't say anything else for a long moment. And then he closed his eyes and swallowed. "My wife was pregnant. She had a rare congenital defect that caused her to hemorrhage."

He swallowed and his skin paled visibly. Sheridan wished she could stop him, wished she could go over and pull his head to her chest and just hold him. But how could she do such a thing when he was talking about the death of a wife and child he'd loved?

"There was nothing the doctors could do. And the baby, who until that time had seemed healthy, was stillborn."

"Oh, Rashid." Her eyes filled with tears. What could

she say? What could she do? His anger over her having a baby for Annie made so much more sense now. He'd talked about risking her life that night. And when she'd asked him what was wrong, he'd told her it was nothing. She'd known it was not nothing.

She hadn't known it was anything so tragic, however.

"Yes, I will love this child. But I'm terrified to do so. Perhaps now you can understand why."

She clasped her hands tight in her lap. "I do."

"Kadir doesn't know about this. No one does. I was in Russia then, running my business, and had very little contact with anyone outside of the microcosm of my life."

It humbled her that he would share something with her that he hadn't even shared with his family. She thought of Emily telling her earlier that Kadir knew something had happened to his brother, but not what. "Maybe you should tell him. Maybe he has words of wisdom that I can't seem to find."

"There are no words of wisdom, Sheridan. You simply get through each day until the pain isn't as great. You never forget, but you learn how to live anyway."

She couldn't sit here any longer and not reach out to him. So she got up and moved closer, taking his hand and squeezing it in hers. That was all. Just a touch. He squeezed back and then they were looking at each other, their gazes tangling, searching, locking together for what seemed forever, but was probably only a few minutes.

"I'm sorry I pried. It wasn't my intention to make you share painful memories."

He lifted her hand to his mouth and kissed her knuckles. "You're very sweet. When you aren't telling me to go to hell, that is."

She smiled. It shook at the corners, but she held it together anyway. "If I didn't tell you, who would? You have far too many people bowing and scraping and bending over backward to serve you. You need someone to remind you that you aren't perfect."

"No, I am definitely not perfect. In this, you are very like Daria."

"That's very sweet of you to say."

"But also mercenary."

"Mercenary?" Her blood beat in her temples, her throat.

His eyes glittered hot. "Life is for the living. And I want you, Sheridan. Now, tonight. I want to take you to my bed and keep you there until you can't move a muscle. Until your body is liquid with pleasure, weak with desire and sated beyond your wildest imaginings."

Her breath caught. "That sounds quite amazing, Your Majesty. But I'm still not certain it's a good idea."

Because he made her heart thrum and her body melt and her eyes sting with tears. She was drawn to him physically, but it was also more than that. And that was what frightened her. How could she spend time with him and not be drawn deeper into that spell? He was so much more than an arrogant and entitled king.

He was a man who'd lived an imperfect life, who'd experienced pain and loss and incredible sadness. He was also lonely, and that loneliness called to her because it was so familiar. He took care of everyone else first—his nation, his duties—and whatever was left over he gave to himself. But it wasn't much.

For a man who was rich in material things, he was sorely lacking in emotional fulfillment.

"We have to start somewhere," he said softly.

Oh, how she wanted to accept, to let him know he didn't need to be alone. But the risk…

"I can't go to bed with you now only to have you freeze me out later."

"I don't want to freeze you out."

"But you do. You have."

"I know."

But he tugged her hand until she had to move right up against him. And then he speared his other hand into her hair and lowered his mouth to hers. She didn't stop him. She closed her eyes, and then his lips met hers and she sighed. He kissed her sweetly, so sweetly, and yet the heat swelled inside her, rolled through her, intensified with each gentle stroke of his tongue against hers.

"I won't get up and go back to my room in the middle of the night," she said between kisses. "I won't, Rashid."

"I understand." And then he kissed her deeper, harder, until the passion unfurled between them, until he pushed her back on the couch and shaped her body with his hands, exploring her curves endlessly.

She thought he would undress her there, but he soon lifted her up and pulled her outside onto the terrace. It was a beautiful night, not too cool yet, with stars winking over the dunes. He took her to the railing and stood there gazing out over the darkened desert. Behind them, the city lights tinted the sky, but it wasn't enough to drown out the vast darkness before them.

"I left Kyr for many years," he said, standing behind her at the railing and putting his arms around her, caging her in. "I gave up the expectation I would become king when I was a young man. I wandered the world, and I started my own business, which I built into the powerful oil company it is today. I became who I am because of my life here in Kyr. And one thing I vowed many years ago was that no child of mine would ever believe I did not love or approve of him. Or her."

He turned her in his arms then and she gazed up at him with eyes blurred with tears. "I believed you the first time you said it," she said softly.

"Yes, but I wanted you to know that I was certain. This child will not lack for love."

Sheridan swallowed the lump in her throat. She wanted to ask him if there could ever be love between them, but she knew it was not a question he wanted to hear. He'd told her he chose not to love, not that he was incapable of it, and so that gave her hope.

She put a hand to his cheek and watched his eyes darken. "You're a good man, Rashid. And I know you'll be a good father."

He turned his head and pressed a kiss into her palm. "You will want for nothing here, *habibti.* I know this is not the life you would have chosen, but I believe you will come to love Kyr as I do."

"I hope I do," she said, her heart pounding at the realization she could love so much more than Kyr if he would let her.

He kissed her suddenly. And this time he did not stop. This time, he kissed her until she was melting and pliant, and then he swept her into his arms—how many times had he done this now, and why did it thrill her every time he did?—and carried her into his bedroom, where he undressed her slowly, kissing and caressing each bit of skin he revealed, until she was quivering with anticipation, until she was ready to beg him for release.

He made love to her first with his mouth, and then, when she was sated and shattered, he settled between her thighs and entered her on a breath-stealing plunge. Sheridan wrapped her legs around him as he rode her, arched her body into his and let him take her over the edge of passion and into the depths of a pleasure so intense it made her cry his name again and again.

When she was shattered and spent again, when she couldn't lift a muscle, Rashid found his release in her body. He rolled away from her and she lay there with the cool air wafting over her heated skin and her brain racing, wondering if he would get up and hand her the clothing he'd dropped onto the floor.

She didn't dare reach out to him. Long minutes passed in which she worried and wondered and thought of what she would say if he withdrew again. And then she thought maybe she should just get up and go. Take the decision away from him. Show him she didn't care about his rejection.

Sheridan pushed herself upright and swung her legs off the bed. She fumbled for her clothes in the dark, her eyes stinging, as Rashid didn't say a word. He didn't care if she left. After everything he'd said, he didn't even care.

But then he was there, his hand smoothing over the curve of her back, her buttock, and she stopped what she was doing as her skin reacted with the same predictable flare of heat as always. Oh, it wasn't fair. It just wasn't fair.

"Don't go," he said. And then he pulled her down, into his arms, and she was lost all over again.

CHAPTER TWELVE

HE'D BEEN RIGHT about her, Rashid thought. She *was* a people pleaser. Sheridan was the kind of bright, sunny sort of person that he was not and never had been. She was light to his dark, sweet to his sour, sunshine to his ice. She made people happy. She spoke with everyone she met as if she was genuinely interested in them. She had to have a translator, but she was beginning to learn a few words and when she tried them out, no matter how badly she mangled them, even the council smiled indulgently.

He did not fool himself that would last, however. The council would eventually begin to demand he take a second wife. He'd told them he would, but he was in no hurry to do so.

Besides, when would he have time for another woman? He was busy enough with Sheridan. Not that she demanded his time, but he often found himself giving it. He went looking for her during the day, found her with her secretary or in the kitchen. Occasionally, he found her in the stables with the puppies.

He looked down at the basket that Mostafa had placed silently beside his desk and took a moment to wonder at himself. Was he going soft?

Soon there was a knock on his door, and Sheridan breezed into the room. She was wearing cream trousers and a red shirt today, and her hair tumbled in blond curls over her shoulders. She was fresh and pretty and glowing.

He glanced at her belly worriedly, but then he told himself it was silly. She wasn't even showing yet. There was nothing to worry about.

"You wanted to see me?" she said.

He stood and went to her side. "I did." He leaned in and kissed her cheek. And then he had to tell himself it was the middle of the day and he had appointments in a few minutes. But he was already hard. It surprised him how quickly she got to him.

As if she knew what kind of internal battle he was having, she slid her arms around him and brought her body against his.

"You smell good, Rashid."

"Stop flirting with me." He tried to sound stern but she only laughed. And then she stood on tiptoe and pulled his head down. He thought she was going to kiss him on the mouth, but she turned her head at the last moment and landed a kiss on his jaw. Then she laughed and pulled out of his arms.

He snatched her back and kissed her properly until she clung to him, until her body went soft and her tongue glided against his and she sighed.

He considered taking her on the desk when there was a noise. A whimper. Sheridan pushed him away and stood with her eyes wide. "What was that?"

"What was what?"

"That…that sound. Like a puppy—" And then her breath caught and her eyes brightened and Rashid reached for the basket. He opened the lid and a pale golden puppy sat there, blinking and yawning.

When it saw Sheridan, the little tail thumped. Sheridan squealed as she reached into the basket and took the puppy out. "Oh, sweet baby, what are you doing in the big, bad king's office? Are you hiding?"

She looked up at him, her eyes shining, and he couldn't remember why he wasn't supposed to feel a flood of warmth at that look. Why it was dangerous to do so.

"The puppies are old enough to go to permanent homes now. I thought you might like one of your own. Daoud said this one was your favorite."

"Oh, Rashid." She bent her head and put her face in the dog's fur. "Yes," she said softly. "He's a precious little guy."

Rashid was beginning to feel uncomfortable. Not in a bad way, but in a "what the hell do I do now" way. Why hadn't he just sent Daoud to her room with the puppy? Except that she wasn't staying in her room lately, was she?

No, she'd been in his every night for the past two weeks. He liked having her there. He thought back to that very first night when he'd found her on his terrace and made love to her. And then he'd jumped out of bed like he'd been singed and escorted her back to her room. He'd followed it up by doing the same thing the next time he'd lost control with her, and she'd thought that meant he didn't want to be touched.

Nothing was further from the truth. He loved when she touched him, loved the tenderness in her fingers, the sweetness in her tongue, the wickedness in her mouth when she took him between her lips. He was beginning to crave her touch.

She beamed at him, her sweet face lighting up with joy. His heart, that organ that was supposed to be encased in ice, kicked. He reached down deep, searching for the ice, jerked it back into place like a blanket.

He could smile, he could be warm and make love, but he could not let his heart be touched. That was the last battleground and the one he would not allow to be breached.

Rashid reached out and stroked the dog's head. "It will be good for the baby to grow up with a dog."

Her smile didn't waver. "It will be good for me, too. Thank you."

She stood on tiptoe to kiss him and then she wandered over to the seating area and set the dog on the floor. The little guy scampered around happily, and Rashid hoped he didn't pee on the rug.

"Are you prepared for the trip?" he asked. They were traveling out into the desert so that he could fulfill his duties to meet with some of the nomadic tribes that still ranged the vast Kyrian Desert. It was mostly ceremonial, but necessary. And while he could leave Sheridan behind for the week or so he would be gone, he wanted her to see the desert as he saw it. The beauty, the majesty, the overwhelming might of all that sand and sun. He wanted his child to feel it inside the womb, to become one with the land, the same as he was.

"I think so. My secretary has been telling me what to expect and what to take."

"How is Layla working out for you?"

He'd sent her a woman who'd trained in European universities and who had a fresh, open manner. Not that he supposed Sheridan would have had any trouble if Layla had been dour, considering how she'd wound Daoud around her finger. If Daoud didn't have a fiancée he adored, Rashid might be jealous.

"I like her. She never makes me feel stupid for not knowing what I'm supposed to do."

Layla had been teaching her protocol and schooling her on Kyrian history in preparation for their upcoming public wedding. Rashid had pushed that out as far as he could, simply because he hadn't wanted to deal with a long day of ceremony and pomp, but the day would arrive soon enough and they'd have to give the Kyrian people something to celebrate.

"I'm glad to hear it."

She frowned a little then. "I asked Annie and Chris if they would come for the formal wedding, but I don't think Annie wants to come."

"I'm sorry, Sheridan." He was predisposed to dislike her sister simply because the other woman seemed not to care how her actions hurt Sheridan, but he knew that it wasn't quite as simple as that. Annie was shy and frightened of new situations. He understood that now, but it didn't mean he liked the way it affected Sheridan.

"I knew it was a long shot. All the pomp and noise, the dignitaries, the heat and strangeness of a place she's never been. It would be too much for her."

He didn't point out that apparently the strangeness of Switzerland, where Annie would have her experimental treatment to try to give her a chance to conceive, didn't seem to bother her.

"We will bring them here another time, then. I will make it happen, I assure you."

She laughed. "Please tell me you're not going to kidnap my sister and her husband, Rashid. If you keep snatching people from the States, eventually you'll be caught, and then there'll be an international incident."

He came and sat down beside her while the puppy yipped and tried to chase his tail. "I won't kidnap them."

"Well, that's a relief."

He tugged her onto his lap because he couldn't quite control himself.

"But I'm not sorry I kidnapped you," he told her, pushing her blond hair back behind her ears and watching the way her eyes darkened with passion as he ghosted a thumb over one budding nipple.

Her voice was a purr. "I thought you had appointments?"

"I'm the king. I can reschedule if I want to." He reached for his phone and punched a button. Mostafa answered. "Reschedule everything for the next two hours."

Sheridan laughed as he tossed the phone aside again. "Such a bossy man. And so certain of yourself. What if I have appointments?"

He pulled her head down to his. "None are more important than this one."

Her mouth brushed his softly, sweetly, and his groin tightened.

"No," she agreed. "None are."

The car that would take Sheridan to her doctor's appointment was waiting for her the next morning. Daoud escorted her down the steps and out the door, but before he could help her into the car Rashid strode outside, looking regal and magnificent in his desert robes.

"I thought you had a meeting," Sheridan said.

Rashid grinned at her. "Did I not explain to you how this works? I am the king. I can reschedule meetings."

Sheridan settled onto the seat and Rashid climbed in beside her. Then the door sealed shut and the car started toward the city.

"It's not necessary for you to be there the first time."

He took her hand in his and butterflies soared in her belly. "I know you're trying to spare me any pain, but I feel as if I should be there for you."

Sheridan's heart squeezed tight as she gazed up at his handsome face. She'd spent every night for the past two weeks in his bed, and she still felt the same butterflies whenever he touched her. Butterflies, heat, need and a melting, aching, wonderful tension that suffused her whole being as he worshipped her body with his own.

And now he'd given her a dog. She'd named the little guy Leo because it just seemed to fit. He was the same tawny gold as a lion, plus he'd been given to her by the Lion of Kyr. Her husband. She dropped her gaze to their linked hands and felt a bittersweet happiness flood her.

Because she was falling for this man. So very hard. Sometimes she thought he cared about her, too, but then she'd catch him standing on the terrace in the middle of the night, leaning against the railing, caught up in thought. She didn't disturb him. She just watched and waited and when she couldn't stay awake any longer, she fell asleep in his bed alone. He never left her right after they made love anymore, but he did leave. Often.

And it hurt. She could admit that to herself. It hurt that he still felt the need to get away from her. She could never understand the depth of the loss he'd experienced, but he couldn't live his life mired in the past. That wasn't good for him. Or for their child.

Or for her, but then she felt as if that was a selfish thought to have. She knew she was not a replacement for his lost wife, a woman he'd loved very much, according to Daoud.

Daoud didn't talk about his king often, and never about anything private, but he had once let it slip to Sheridan that he'd been with Rashid in Russia and that he'd watched him change after the tragedy. Rashid had never been a bubbly person, but he'd closed down completely in the aftermath of his wife and child's death.

Sheridan squeezed Rashid's hand and hoped he didn't regret coming with her today.

They soon arrived at the Royal Kyrian Hospital and were ushered into a spotless examining room. There was no such thing as waiting to be seen when you were the king of Kyr, because the doctor and her staff were already there and waiting for Sheridan to arrive.

After being directed to change and then ushered onto the table, Sheridan lay there while the doctor used the ultrasound wand to search for a heartbeat. Rashid stood beside her, holding her hand, his eyes on the screen as the doctor found the tiny bean that was their baby.

And then the heartbeat filled the speaker and Sheridan couldn't contain a sob. She bit her lip, trembling from head to toe, while the doctor took photos. Rashid's grip tightened. She looked up at him, at the whiteness of his skin, and her heart skipped.

He was reliving an earlier moment just like this, she imagined, and she wished she could tell him it was okay, that it would all be okay. But she couldn't really guarantee such a thing, could she?

The doctor said something in Arabic that suddenly

had Rashid's fingers tightening even more. The wand stopped moving and the doctor stared at the screen.

"Twins," she said after a long moment. She turned to look at Sheridan. "You are having twins, Your Highness."

Rashid stood looking at the screen, his body as rigid as a board. "Twins? You are certain?"

The doctor smiled. "Yes, Your Majesty. There are two heartbeats." She turned the sound on again. And Sheridan could hear it, the faint beat of another heart beneath the pounding of the first.

"They're so fast," Sheridan said, worried at the quick tempo.

"This is perfectly normal," the doctor replied.

She finished up the exam and then they discussed things like vitamins, exercise and birthing classes. It all seemed so surreal to Sheridan. When it was finally over, the staff made another appointment for her and then she and Rashid were back in the car and returning to the palace.

The silence between them was uncomfortably thick. Sheridan searched for things to say, but discarded most of them. What did you say to a man who was staring out the window and ignoring you after hearing the heartbeats of his children? If he was any other man, she might ask him what was wrong.

But she knew, didn't she? It was the ones who didn't make it, the ones he'd loved and lost that were on his mind.

"Are you all right?" she finally asked when the silence stretched too thin. Outside the car, life went on as usual, but inside it was quiet and strained.

He turned to look at her. His eyes were bleak. "I'm fine."

"You shouldn't have come."

He was polite and distant at once. "You shouldn't have to go through this alone. I wanted to be there."

"But it causes you pain."

"I've been through this before, Sheridan. I knew what to expect when I went with you."

"You haven't said anything since we heard the heart-beats."

His jaw flexed. "It was a shock. I didn't expect two babies. I don't think you did, either."

"No. But twins run in my family, though in my aunts and cousins, not my mother. I didn't even consider it would happen to me."

His gaze raked her. "You are so slight. Are the other women in your family as small?"

"My Aunt Liz is, yes, and she had twins. No problems other than a bit of preeclampsia at the end." She sighed. "It will be fine, Rashid. What happened to your wife—well, it was uncommon. Tragic and terrible, but uncommon."

He seemed so detached and cold. "I am aware of this."

They reached the palace then and the doors swung open. Rashid helped her out of the car and led her inside while the palace guards saluted and other servants bowed as they passed. Her heart pounded as they walked through the ornate and beautiful corridors. She wanted to rewind the clock, to go back to the way things were before they'd gone to the hospital, but that was impossible now. She simply had to deal with the aloof man at her side and wait for him to thaw again.

When they reached the private wing, he stopped before the door. He looked as if he'd like nothing better than to escape. "The doctor said you should rest."

"Yes, but it's not even lunchtime yet and I just got up a couple of hours ago."

"Still. Two babies will sap your strength if you aren't careful."

"They are the size of beans, Rashid. I think I can handle some activity. Besides, I still have things to do before we go into the desert. Layla has promised to give me some more lessons this morning on protocol. I think it would be wise to learn as much as I can if I'm not to embarrass you out there."

He grew very still then and a tiny thread of unease uncoiled within her. She knew what he would say before he said it. "Perhaps you should not go with me, *habibti*. We'll be moving around a lot. Besides, it's dreadfully hot, and you might get ill. You should stay here and think about the public wedding. There is much to be done yet."

Sheridan put her hand on his arm. He stiffened beneath her touch and she dropped her hand, hurt by his rejection. Frustration pounded into her. She would not be silent.

"Why are you behaving like this? I'm not any *more* pregnant than when we left here this morning. Why is it suddenly too hot for me to go with you?"

He swallowed. "It's not suddenly too hot. It's always been too hot. I failed to consider it before."

Of course she knew what was wrong with him. She'd been worried about it since he'd insisted on going with her to the hospital. How could he contain his anxiety at what might happen to his children when his previous experience had been so tragic?

"So now that you've seen the babies and heard their

heartbeats, it's too hot? What else, Rashid? Is it too dangerous to have sex now, too? Too dark at night, too light during the day, too many steps between the bedroom and the kitchen? Is Leo too energetic for me? Should I lie down in bed and not get out for the next few months?"

She was on the edge of hysteria. She knew it, but she was just so furious. It was like she'd had him for a little while, had the beginnings of such a perfect life going with him, and now he was slipping away. Slipping into the past and the tragedy that had happened to him.

Slipping away from her.

Because he was afraid of caring and afraid of being hurt. Her heart ached so much for him. She wanted to slap him silly and she wanted to hold him close and tell him that he had to learn to feel again. For their family. Because he deserved to know love again.

She wanted him to know that *she* loved him. She couldn't help it. She'd tried not to fall, but how could she not?

The way he touched her, held her, the way he said her name when they were in bed together, and the way he reached out to her when she knew it was a difficult thing for him to do. He had feelings that went deep, and he was terrified of them.

But how could she love a man who didn't love her? How could she watch him with her children and know he would always keep part of himself separate from them?

At this moment, he'd retreated behind his barriers. He was aloof and cool and she wanted to scream.

"Don't be melodramatic, Sheridan," he snapped. "I'm thinking of your health and the babies. There is nothing wrong with this. You should be thankful I give a damn at all."

And that was it, the blow that had her reeling. The metaphorical slap to the face that reminded her of her place and jolted right down to her soul. She knew she wasn't a replacement wife, but she'd hoped—no, she'd begun to believe—that she might mean something to him in her own right.

But this sarcasm, this utter arrogance? She couldn't stomach it, no matter how she ached for him.

"I see," she said, quietly shaking inside. He was stiff and formal now, all trace of the thoughtful lover gone. It hurt so much. She'd be damned if she'd let him see it, though. "Thank you for letting me know. I am so fortunate that you care."

His nostrils flared, a single concession to emotion. She hoped he might break then, hoped he might tell her he was sorry, that he hadn't meant that the way it sounded.

He almost did.

"Sheridan, I—" He stopped, clenched his jaw, shook his head. And then he looked at her again with eyes that were cold and empty. Icy. "Go rest. I'll see you when I return in a week."

CHAPTER THIRTEEN

RASHID HAD BEEN gone for three days when the rumor reached her. Sheridan stared at Fatima and blinked. Hard. Her belly twisted into knots as she asked Fatima to repeat what she'd said.

Fatima didn't seem to hear the note of anxiety in Sheridan's voice.

"There is talk His Majesty will choose a second wife from one of the tribes, Your Highness."

"A second wife." How had she been in Kyr for over a month now and not considered that Rashid could have another wife?

"A Kyrian wife."

"I see." But she didn't. Fatima clearly thought this was not a problem because she went about her work as if she hadn't just upended the foundation of Sheridan's entire being. A second wife. A Kyrian wife. Why hadn't she seen this coming? And why hadn't Rashid told her it was possible?

After they'd returned from the hospital, she'd been angry and hurt by Rashid's sudden distance. But she'd known it would do no good to push him. She had to give him space, had to let him come around to it in his own time. He was an intelligent man and he would eventually realize he couldn't hide from life. He would miss her in his bed and he would want to continue the relationship they'd had. She'd had every faith they would grow together as a couple.

They might not have married for love, but that didn't mean love wouldn't grow.

But what if she was only fooling herself? He'd spent two weeks taking her to his bed every night and making love to her. He'd given her a puppy because he knew she'd never had one. But what else did he do that indicated his feelings for her might evolve?

He'd gone to the hospital with her so he could show his support, but he'd come away more distant than ever.

And now he'd gone into the desert without her. Could he possibly be looking for another wife? It didn't seem plausible, since he'd planned to take her with him up until the last possible moment. Would he really have gone wife shopping with her along?

His mood had changed so drastically after the revelation they were going to have twins that she couldn't be certain what was on his mind anymore. They weren't from the same world, and it certainly wasn't unusual in his to contemplate such a thing.

She grew chilled as she considered what it would mean for Rashid to have another wife. He would take another woman to his bed. Sheridan would have to wait her *turn* to be with him. She would grow big with his children and she would be shunned while he chose to spend his evenings with another.

In spite of the churning of her brain, Sheridan tried to go about the business of helping Layla to plan the wedding ceremony. It was to be a day of celebration in Kyr, a holiday for the people, and no expense was to be spared.

But she kept asking herself if she'd be helping to plan another of these events for Rashid and a second wife. And that was something she could not do. Not ever. Her stomach twisted in on itself until she couldn't even stand the thought of food. She grew shaky and hot and had to go lie down.

But she couldn't really rest. She kept thinking about how much her life had changed, how Rashid had come and snatched her out of Savannah with little thought to what she wanted, and then how he'd managed to woo her with hot kisses and silky caresses. She'd fallen deep under his spell.

But she had to be brutally honest with herself: it wasn't mutual. She wasn't sure it ever would be. And she couldn't live like that. She just couldn't. She was patient and she'd been willing to give him time—but if he brought home another wife? Hot tears fell down her cheeks and she swiped them away angrily.

No. Just *no.*

Sheridan got up and went to wash her face. She changed into a Kyrian dress and covered her hair with a hijab. She wasn't going to sit here and wait for Rashid to return with another woman on his arm. She'd been the good girl for so long. All her life, she'd given up things she wanted so that Annie would be happy.

It was the ultimate irony that she was here with Rashid *because* she'd been trying to make Annie happy. No other reason. And she'd been doing what she always did with loved ones, which was to be supportive and understanding and hope that they could come to happiness on their own. She'd tried to give Annie a baby, and she'd tried to give Rashid time and space.

Nothing she'd done worked. It was time she admitted that. And it was time she stood up for herself. *Past* time. Sheridan was done putting everyone but herself first. It was time she took action.

Time she demanded that Rashid make a choice.

Rashid sat through yet another meeting in yet another desert enclave, listening to his people's concerns and making plans for how to best help them. The nomads weren't quite the same as when he'd been a boy. Now they had generators, televisions, cell phones and satellite dishes. These things brought concerns of their own, so of course he promised to look into them.

And then there were the daughters. At every stop, he was presented with daughters who would, it was hinted, make fine wives. All of Kyr knew of his marriage to Sheridan, and of the upcoming national holiday in celebration. Soon they would announce the impending arrival of the royal twins, but not until Sheridan was safely into the second trimester.

Rashid's teeth ground together at that thought. Was there truly anything quite so ironic as safety during a pregnancy? So many things could go wrong. Babies were fine up until birth, and then they were stillborn. Mothers hemorrhaged to death. Things went wrong.

It made him break out into a cold sweat.

Not because he was in love with Sheridan, but he did like her. Against all his plans otherwise, he liked the woman he'd had to marry. She was so open and giving, so thoughtful. She'd been worried about his reaction at the hospital before anything had happened—and he'd proved her correct, had he not, when he'd been unable to handle the news she was pregnant with twins?

He'd hurt her by being so cold after, but he'd had to

escape. He'd had a sensation very like panic that had wanted to crawl up his throat and wrap its fingers around his neck. He hadn't known what would happen if that was allowed to occur. And so he'd planned his escape. He'd left her there and embarked on his trip without her.

And now he missed her. Missed her sweet scent, her sensual body, her soft hands and wicked tongue. He sat through meetings and pictured her naked, and then he shook his head and forced those thoughts away before he embarrassed himself in front of the tribal chieftains.

At dusk, Rashid returned to the tent they'd set up for him—an opulent tent adorned with the usual beautiful carpets, but also with most of the modern conveniences one would expect in the city, thanks to the generators that hummed efficiently nearby.

Rashid peeled off his head covering and shrugged out of the long robe, leaving only the light trousers beneath. Maybe he should call Sheridan, see how she was faring. He'd had reports from Mostafa that all was well with her, and the tight knot around his heart had slowly begun to ease.

He would go back to the palace in four days, and he would no doubt take her to his bed again. But he wouldn't let himself forget there were consequences to allowing a woman to get too close. Not ever again.

Yet part of him chafed at that restriction. Finally, he reached for his phone, determined to call her and see how she was doing.

But it rang right as he was about to dial. He answered to find a very breathless Mostafa on the other end. "Your Majesty," he said, and Rashid could hear the panic in his voice. The thread of utter chaos running through that familiar baritone.

Ice water ran in his veins then, flooding him with that familiar calm before the storm. "What is it, Mostafa?"

"Her Highness," he began, and Rashid's gut twisted. "She is gone."

Rashid was tempted to take the phone from his head and stare at it, but instead he forced himself to be cool. "What do you mean gone, Mostafa? Has she left the palace to go shopping? Gone to the airport in order to run away? Or is she hiding in the stables, perhaps?"

"She took a horse, Your Majesty."

Rashid blinked. "A horse?" Had Mostafa lost his mind? Had Sheridan? "Where is Daoud?"

"He is gone, too. When we discovered Her Highness had left on horseback, he went after her."

Daoud and Sheridan were on horseback. In the Kyrian Desert. But for what purpose? Why had Sheridan done such a thing? To get his attention? To bring him back to her side? The fear he'd tried to keep at bay broke through his barriers and flooded his system like a swirling tornado of sand. It scoured through him, raked him bare and filled him with utter dread.

And fury.

She'd taken a horse. She was pregnant and she'd taken a horse. Climbed on top of its back and rode it into the desert. Why? Why?

And then realization hit him. Hard. What if she wanted to harm herself? The desert was dangerous and she'd gone into it alone. Had he pushed her to the edge? Was she trying to get his attention—or trying to end her life?

That thought made the ice in his veins harder than ever—but for a different reason. He couldn't imagine Sheridan gone from his life. Couldn't imagine waking up without her in this world, without her smile or her touch or the look in her eyes when he entered her body and then took her with him to paradise.

She wasn't Daria but she was…she was *Sheridan.* And Sheridan meant something to him. She really meant something….

He was still reeling from the realization that he cared, that he'd not insulated himself from a damn thing by running away from her, that he couldn't control his emotions as if they had an on/off switch the way he'd always believed, when Mostafa said something that made his gut turn to stone.

Mostafa was talking about a search party and the coming night—and a thunderstorm.

A thunderstorm. Sandstorms in the desert were bad enough, but rain was the true danger. It was such a rare occurrence that when it happened, the rain created floods in the wadis—and the sand turned to sludge. Sludge that could trap anything in its path and annihilate it.

Rain was the true enemy of the desert, and a woman alone on a horse in unfamiliar territory—even if she did survive the brutality of a night exposed to the cold and sand, the jackals and scorpions and lions—was no match for a thunderstorm.

Rashid dressed quickly and then strode from the tent, calling orders as he went. Someone saddled a horse at the same time the Bedouin men emerged from their tents where they'd been preparing for dinner. Rashid and two dozen other men swung into saddles simultaneously. Arabian horses pranced and pawed and snorted, but ultimately they were ready for a ride into the night.

Sheridan could be anywhere out there, but Rashid

knew the direction of the city and he knew the most traveled routes. All who were raised in the desert did. Rashid spurred his horse into a gallop and twenty-four men did the same. It was still light, though only barely, the sky a pink stain across the horizon. The moon was full tonight and they would have it for a couple of hours once it rose, until the predicted storm swept in off the gulf and wreaked its havoc.

Rashid only prayed they would find Sheridan before that happened. Because if they did not, if she had to endure a storm in the desert alone… His breath caught painfully in his lungs as the truth hit him full force: if they did not find her soon, there was no way she would survive.

It had seemed like such a good idea at the time, Sheridan thought. She'd been going to the stables so often that no one had thought anything of it when she went again. Even Daoud had relaxed his guard because he was accustomed to her visiting the stables. There were still a couple of the puppies who were waiting for their forever homes, and she wouldn't stop playing with them just because Rashid had given her Leo.

It had been ridiculously easy to saddle a horse and ride out of the barn. She hadn't been thinking too much at the time, but she'd known from listening in the palace that the Bedouin were only a few hours away by horseback. Had she really thought she could ride out to the oasis and find Rashid?

Fatima had told her he was in a place called the King's Oasis, and she'd described it in great detail. Sheridan wasn't an idiot. She had a map and a compass—handy devices, those, and still quite necessary. She'd located one in the palace after a bit of inquiry. All smartphones had them these days, but of course there were battery and satellite issues to contend with.

So now she was riding along a ridge on a delicate Arabian mare, with the desert a sea of sand in front of her and the city a speck behind her, and beginning to come to her senses. Not only that, but darkness was also falling fast and she had no idea how she was supposed to keep riding in the night. To her left, there was a dark wall of clouds in the distance, and she didn't know if they were headed her way or not. They looked ominous, though, like thunderheads off the coast in Savannah.

The occasional brightening of those clouds told her that was exactly what they were as lightning sizzled through them and painted parts of the bank white and pink. She'd never realized there were thunderstorms in this area of the world, but why wouldn't there be? Her only comfort was that this was a desert and therefore they would lose their destructive power long before they arrived. Or so she thought, since a desert by definition was dry.

She was tempted to turn around, but the compass told her she had gone past the point of no return. If she stayed on track, she would reach the oasis in two more hours.

And Rashid would blow a gasket. Sheridan sank into the saddle as she imagined his face when he saw her. At first, she'd thought she would ride in like a general at the head of the army, triumphant and oozing righteousness. Now she imagined she would limp in like a worn-out puppy, her tail between her legs and her body aching from the punishment of a long ride.

In another hour, it was completely dark, except for the silver light of the moon painting the dunes. It was gorgeous and wild out here and Sheridan was at least partly enchanted by the beauty. But she was also worried, because the clouds were drawing ever closer. The moon would be blotted out before long, and while the flashing in the clouds would give light, it was a lot more worrisome the closer they got.

Not to mention the sand was beginning to blow in gusts, stinging her exposed skin. The horse trudged along sure footedly, but Sheridan wasn't certain how much longer that could last. She'd been so stupid. She'd behaved impulsively, rashly, and Rashid was going to be ashamed of her.

She could hear thunder in the clouds now—and something else. Something that set the hair on the back of her neck prickling. There was a howl somewhere to her right. And then another howl behind her. The horse snorted and kicked up her heels, and Sheridan snatched at the reins, desperate to keep the mare from bolting.

And then something snarled nearby and there was the sound of many animals moving at once. The mare tossed her head and reared onto her hind legs—and then she bolted forward while Sheridan cried out and tried to wrap her hands into the mare's mane.

But she'd been caught by surprise and she couldn't hold on. She fell to the sand with a scream.

CHAPTER FOURTEEN

THE ANIMALS BORE down on her quickly, snarling and thumping and snorting, and Sheridan rolled into a ball and tried to protect her head. She would die out here in the Kyrian Desert, her babies with her, and all because she'd been so tormented over a man that she'd lost her head.

There was another howl, and a shriek that was quickly cut off. And then the thumping grew louder and Sheridan realized there was shouting. Men shouting. She was afraid to uncoil her body, just in case the beasts were still there, but then she felt rough hands on her. She didn't even scream as a man jerked her up and against his body. He called out in rough Arabic and then she was flung onto a horse and the man climbed up behind her.

The hijab had fallen around her eyes and she couldn't see anything at all, but there was a man and a horse and she hung on to his waist for dear life as the horse bolted forward into the night. Around them, she thought she heard more hooves, more horses, but the sound became a dull throbbing as thunder split the night.

And then she felt the first cold drops of rain on her back and head. She was stunned as the rain began to fall harder. She would have never guessed. But the wind howled and the horses ran and the rain fell, and Sheridan had no idea where she was or who she was with.

But since the man was infinitely preferable to the beasts, whatever they were, she was grateful for the moment just to be where she was.

They rode for what seemed forever, the rain pounding down, the wind whipping, the horses straining forward, until finally they came to an abrupt halt and Sheridan knocked her head on the man's chest.

There was more Arabic ringing through the night, and then another man put hands around her waist and helped her down. The man on the horse followed, and then he swept her into his arms as if she was a rag doll and strode into a tent. Sheridan struggled to push the fabric from her face. Her teeth were chattering and her skin prickled with goose bumps.

The man dumped her unceremoniously onto her feet and began to remove her clothing. That was when Sheridan came to her senses. She batted at his hands and tried to scramble away. He said something, but the blood rushing in her ears prevented her from understanding. She just knew she had to get away from him. She had to find Rashid.

She drew in breath to scream—

And the man jerked her into his arms, his mouth coming roughly down on top of hers, silencing her.

Sheridan struggled for only a moment before she realized whose mouth was ravaging hers, whose arms wrapped around her, whose hands speared into her hair and tilted her head back for greater access.

She clung to him, her body softening, hands clutching his wet robes. When he realized she knew, he set her away from him, though she whimpered and wanted to stay in his arms.

"We have to get you out of that wet clothing, *habibti*," he said, his voice rough and beautiful.

Her teeth were chattering again and this time when he began to strip her, she didn't stop him. Her hands were too cold to help and so she simply stood there while he stripped the clothing from her body and then wrapped her in a warm blanket. He chafed her arms and then he picked her up and carried her to the bed, where he set her down and pulled a soft fur on top of her.

"Rashid," she said when he started to walk away, but he only turned and shot her a look that she couldn't read.

He was wet, too, his hair sticking to his head, his face streaked with moisture. He did not seem to be as cold as she was, however.

"I'm going to send for something hot to drink. I'm not leaving."

When he walked out, she huddled under the blankets, her brain whirling. She'd made a grave mistake coming here like this. He would be furious, and he would think her unbalanced for even attempting such a crazy thing. Why wouldn't he want another wife? A more sensible one who didn't act on her emotions without fully considering her actions first?

He returned soon with a brass pot and two cups. He poured tea for her, laced it with sugar and handed her a cup.

"I'm afraid the Bedouin don't drink decaffeinated tea, but this is weak. It shouldn't hurt the babies."

She dropped her eyes as she studied the cup, blowing on the steam curling over the top of the liquid. Shame rolled through her.

She could hear him pouring tea for himself, stirring the tiny spoon against the glass, and her nerves tightened as she waited for the explosion.

When it didn't come, she looked up and met a hot, dark gaze staring back at her. Her heart turned over.

"I'm sorry," she said. "I shouldn't have left the palace."

"No, you shouldn't have." He lifted his cup and she thought his hands were shaking, but then she decided it was just her who was shaking. "You could have died out there, Sheridan. The desert is very unforgiving."

"I know."

Strong fingers suddenly gripped her chin and lifted her face until she had to look directly at him again. His gaze was searching.

"Is that what you wanted to do?"

She blinked. "Wh-what?" It took her a moment to process it, but when she did, she sucked in a hard breath. "God, no! I wasn't trying to kill myself!"

"Then what were you doing?" He sounded angry now. Harsh. "Because you almost did just that, *habibti!* You and the babies were moments away from being mauled by jackals. If we had not come along when we did—"

The color drained from his face and he closed his eyes, his jaw tight.

At that look on his face, there was nothing she could do but tell him the truth. The reason she'd set out on a journey toward this oasis in the first place. Besides, she was too weary to dance around the subject any longer.

"I heard you were going to bring home another wife."

His head snapped up then, his black gaze boring into her. "Where did you hear this?"

"In the palace. The rumor is that you will marry one

of the chieftains' daughters." She lifted her chin. "I know that's not unusual in Kyr, but it's unusual for me."

"And so you decided to risk your life, and the lives of our children, to make your opinion known? Did it not occur to you to ask me about this when I returned?"

She snorted. "With a new wife on your arm? No, it didn't occur to me to wait."

"Sheridan." He shook his head. Said something in Arabic. And then he was looking at her again, his eyes filled with fury. "This stubbornness of yours could have cost you your life!"

"I realize that now!" she shouted back. "I behaved stupidly, I know it, and you're embarrassed and furious and no doubt the new wife is signing documents as we speak. Well, I won't live like that! I can't."

She put a fist to her heart, felt hot tears begin to roll down her cheeks and cursed herself for being so damned emotional. *Hormones,* she reminded herself.

"I won't do it, Rashid."

He looked stunned. "You do realize I am the king? That it's not your place to advise me on this?"

The trembling in her limbs was no longer only due to the cold. "Just tell me if it's true. Are you planning to take another wife?"

His jaw was marble. "Kyrian politics are complicated, Sheridan."

"That's not an answer." Her voice was a painful whisper over the lump in her throat.

He closed his eyes and put his forehead in his palm. "The council wishes me to take a Kyrian wife. But I did not come out here to do that."

"And yet it's only a matter of time."

"It would seem so."

She sipped the tea as if they were having a polite conversation rather than one that broke her heart and ripped out her guts.

"Well, thank you for being honest. If you could perhaps wait until the babies are born, I'll be busy enough then that I won't mind so much."

He growled. "You won't *mind* so much?"

She looked at him evenly, though her face was still hot with tears. "As you've taken pains to inform me from the beginning, I have no choice. And no say in the matter, either. If you take another wife, I'll endeavor not to disembowel you both with Daoud's sword."

If Rashid was amused or alarmed, he didn't show it. "He followed you, you know."

She didn't, but her heart skipped a beat at the thought of Daoud out there alone, too. Guilt filled her then. And fear. "Is he all right? The jackals didn't get him, did they?"

"He is fine. His horse went lame, which is why he didn't catch you. I sent men after him once we found you. They returned a few moments ago, and Daoud is well. For the moment."

She heard the dangerous note in his voice. "Rashid, it's not his fault. He trusted me and I gave him the slip."

"He should not have trusted you at all."

"Maybe not." She bowed her head. "Probably not."

"Apparently I should not, either. Or at least not with any swords."

She glared at him. "Are you making fun of me?"

"I'd rather do something else with you."

She sat there in shock for a moment. And then she shook her head violently. "No. I can't. Not ever again, Rashid. Not if you're going to marry another woman."

He reached for her, gripped her chin and forced her to look at him again. His eyes were bright. "Why not, *habibti?* Why would this bother you? Is it because you are American? Or is there another reason?"

Her heart thrummed and her throat ached and she wanted to sink beneath the covers and hide. He was holding her, demanding an answer, and all she could think was that she wanted him to kiss her. And then she wanted to strangle him.

"I've grown fond of you," she said as primly as she could manage under the circumstances. It was such a bald-faced lie, but she'd die before she'd admit that she loved him now.

She did not expect him to grin. "Fond? I like the sound of that."

She swatted at his hand. "I meant to say I *was* fond of you. I've changed my mind now. Who could be fond of a dictator?"

He took her teacup and set it aside. Then he moved closer, threaded his hand through her still-damp hair. "Who indeed?"

His head descended and she closed her eyes, aching for his kiss. But a hot feeling swelled inside her, bubbling up until she put her hand over his mouth and stopped him from kissing her. If he kissed her, she would sob her heart out and confess all her tragic feelings for him.

And she couldn't do that and keep her dignity.

"No, Rashid. You kiss me and charm me and make me forget myself, but this is where it has to stop. I can't do this anymore. I can't be with a man who runs away from his feelings, a man who can't even be with me without wanting to escape. I can't give you everything I have and only get part of you in return. I've spent too much of my life making other people happy and I'm not going to keep doing it with you when you can't even give me something so basic as a normal marriage between two people. I deserve better than that. I *demand* better than that."

She took her hand away slowly, expecting him to explode in arrogant pronouncements about being a king and her having a place, but he caught her hand and held it in his. His skin burned into her. She wanted to pull her hand away and she wanted to curl into his heat at once.

Why did she have to love a man who was so wrong for her on so many levels?

His brows drew together as he studied her. And then he lifted a finger and traced her mouth lightly, so lightly. She refused to whimper.

"When Mostafa called to say you were missing, I thought I was about to relive that moment when I lost Daria and our son. And I was terrified, but not because of what happened in the past and how much it hurt."

He pulled in a deep breath, his nostrils flaring. "I was terrified because it could happen again, and it would hurt just as much this time as the last. It would hurt because of you, Sheridan."

Tears filled her eyes then, but she shook her head and wished she could plug her ears. Because the beautiful words didn't mean what she so desperately wished they meant. They couldn't. Could they?

"Don't say that, Rashid. Don't say things like that to me when you intend to marry someone else someday."

He held her hard against him and she could feel his heart beating strong and fast. "I don't intend to marry anyone else, *habibti*. I said the council wishes it. I even agreed to it because it made political sense, but I am the king and I can change my mind. And I have changed my mind, Sheridan. I don't want any woman but you. I won't have any woman in my bed but you. You're all I need. You and our children."

Sheridan's fingers curled into his damp clothes as she squeezed her eyes tight shut and held on. It was as if she'd suddenly gotten onto a crazy merry-go-round and she couldn't get off. She was dizzy with the feelings ricocheting through her and confused about what was happening.

She pushed away from him until she could see his eyes. "What does this mean, Rashid? I need you to say it plainly. I need to understand."

He pushed the damp hair off her face. He looked so serious. So worried. "It means that I tried to harden my heart against you, but I failed. It means that I'm terrified about you carrying two babies, and that as much as I might like to spank you right now for what you did tonight, I'd much rather fall to my knees and worship your body and thank Allah that you are mine. It means that I love you, Sheridan, though I tried not to. I'm finished with running from this thing between us."

The lump in her throat was huge. "This thing between us?"

He laughed softly. "Have you not noticed? It's incendiary. I touch you, you touch me, and the room goes up in flame. But it's not just sex, Sheridan. I've had sex before, and it doesn't feel quite like that. With you, I can't get enough. Not just of sex, but of you. When I'm not with you, I want to be. And when I am with you, I want to be closer. I know you feel these things, too. You would have to in order to put up with me these past few weeks."

She smoothed her hand over his chest. "Oh, Rashid,

just when I think you can't say anything else that surprises me, you say this. I thought it was just me who couldn't get enough. I thought I was weak where you were concerned and I kept telling myself I needed to be stronger, that I should tell you no. But I couldn't."

"You haven't said you love me, *habibti.*" He ran his fingers over her cheek. "And you don't have to. I already know. And if I had any doubts before, the fact you risked your life to come out here because of a rumor would have erased them all. I'm still angry with you for this, by the way. You should have called me."

"I wasn't sure you wouldn't run away from the question. I had to see your eyes."

He sighed. "Yes, I understand. But never do this again. If you had perished out there—" He swallowed hard. "I would have perished with you, Sheridan. Do you understand that? I would have perished, too."

Tears slid down her cheeks again, only this time she felt free enough to lean forward and kiss him. He was hers, really hers, and she wasn't hiding her feelings another moment. He caught her to him again and kissed her until she was on fire. She was no longer cold, but burning up from the inside out, her entire being filled with flame.

Somehow they got him out of his damp clothing and then he was under the furs with her, their hot limbs tangling together as they rolled together beneath the covers. She ended up on top, straddling him, sinking down on top of him until they both groaned with the rightness of it.

"Sheridan," he gasped, gazing up at her, his expression filled with so much more than simply heat.

She lowered her mouth to his, kissed him tenderly,

teasing it out until neither of them could stand it a moment longer. He gripped her hips and drove up into her while she rode him faster and faster.

They came together, gasping and crying out as the flame rolled through them. And then they collapsed into each other's arms with soft caresses and even softer kisses.

"I love you, Rashid," she said shyly, and he squeezed her tight. She could feel his smile against her hair.

"I love you, too, Sheridan. You keep me grounded."

"You mean I keep your ego in check," she said, laughing.

"That, too." He stroked his fingers up and down her arm. "I didn't know how lost I was until you entered my life."

"And I didn't know I would find home with a man who lived in such a different world than my own. But I did."

"Do you like it here?" he asked, and she thought he seemed a little hesitant. As if it worried him.

"I love it more every day. But the truth is I would love any place in this world so long as you were there. *You* are my home. You."

He squeezed her to him and they said nothing for a long while. But then they began to talk and they spent the evening speaking softly about so many things, and then they made love again, tenderly, before falling asleep curled tightly together.

They would return to the city in a few days and Rashid would issue the proclamation, at their public wedding ceremony, that Sheridan was to be his queen and not just a princess consort. He would deal with the council and they would learn to be happy. In time, they would come to love Queen Sheri, as they called her, as fiercely as if she had been born one of their own.

But tonight was precisely how the royal couple would spend every night for the rest of their lives. Curled together, complete in each other. First, last and always.

EPILOGUE

TWINS. RASHID STILL couldn't believe it, though he'd known for months they were coming. Sheridan had gotten huge and he'd worried himself silly, but his babies were born—a boy and a girl named Tarek and Amira—and his wife was safe. He watched her sleeping now, her hand held lightly in his as she rested after the long ordeal of giving birth.

Eventually her eyes fluttered open and found his. And then she smiled and his whole world lit up from within.

"Habibti," he said, his voice choked with emotion. Such incredible emotion. He'd never thought he could love so deeply more than once in a lifetime. But he did. He'd experienced it numerous times now, he realized. His wife. His children.

He was a lucky, lucky man.

"Have you been here long?" she asked.

He pressed his lips to her hand, her palm to his cheek, and reached forward to slide his fingers over her jaw. "Every moment."

Her eyes widened then. "Rashid! You have to get some rest. Go to the adjoining room and sleep. That's why they prepared this suite for us after all. So the king could rest with his wife in the hospital."

"I couldn't leave you."

Her smile was tender. "It's okay, Rashid. I'm not going anywhere. I plan to hang around and give you hell for the rest of your life. And I plan to give you more babies, too. Though maybe we'd better get used to two for right now."

His throat was tight. She understood his fears and knew just what to say to him. "I love you, Sheridan."

Her eyes were soft and filled with love. For him. It continually astounded him. "I love you, too, arrogant man. Now go and sleep for a while."

"I napped here in the chair. I'm fine. I also have some news for you."

Her gaze sparkled with interest. "What kind of news?"

"Your brother-in-law called."

Her eyes lit up with hope. "And?"

"The twenty-week scan shows a girl. A healthy girl."

Her eyes squeezed tightly shut. "Oh, thank God."

"He says your sister is very happy and she looks forward to talking to you when you feel up to it."

She pushed herself upright, wincing only a little. "I feel up to it now. What time is it?"

He almost laughed. "It's the middle of the night in Georgia. I think you need to wait a few more hours."

She sank back down again. "If I must."

"Kadir and Emily arrived a few hours ago. They're resting in the palace, but they will come by and visit soon."

Sheridan smiled. "I can't wait to see them."

"I believe they have some news to share, as well."

Her eyes widened. "Is Emily pregnant? Oh, that's so wonderful!"

He laughed at the way she didn't even let him answer the question before she exclaimed it was wonderful. "I did not confirm this to you, but yes. Kadir told me that Emily wanted to tell you herself, so you will act surprised."

"I promise I will."

There was a knock on the door and a nurse came in. "Your Majesty, are you ready for the babies? They're awake and hungry."

Sheridan's face lit up. "Yes, please, bring them here."

Two nurses came in and gently placed little Tarek and Amira on Sheridan's lap. Rashid watched his wife settle down with their children and his heart filled with emotion. He'd never thought he would experience this kind of utter happiness in his life, but he was so grateful he'd been given the chance. It continually astounded him that he had been.

When the twins were content and starting to sleep, Sheridan looked up at him, her eyes filled with love. "Would you like to hold one of them?"

Fear crowded him then, but he sucked in a breath, determined to be brave for his family. "Yes, I will do this."

She laughed. "You'll be a natural, Rashid. And you have to start some time."

He reached down and picked up a baby—he didn't know which one—and held it close to his chest, making sure to support the head the way he'd been told. The little face was pinched tight, the eyes closed, but the tiny creature's chest rose and fell regularly and the little lips moved.

"I don't know which one this is," he said softly, gazing with wonder at the baby and not wanting to wake it.

Sheridan laughed again. "That's Tarek. See the blue band on his little wrist?"

"Tarek." Rashid could only stare at the sweet little face. And then he lifted the baby higher and pressed a kiss to his cheek. "My son."

* * * * *

Available July 15, 2014

#3257 BILLIONAIRE'S SECRET

The Chatsfield

by Chantelle Shaw

Sophie Ashdown must lure tormented soul Nicolo Chatsfield from his family's crumbling estate to attend the shareholders' meeting. A glimmer of hope in the shadows of Nicolo's lonely world, Sophie soon finds herself under the spell of this darkly compelling Chatsfield!

#3258 ZARIF'S CONVENIENT QUEEN

The Legacies of Powerful Men

by Lynne Graham

Prince Zarif al Rastani once broke Ella Gilchrist's heart. For the sake of his country this ex-playboy now needs a bride, so when Ella returns begging for his help to rescue her family from ruin, Zarif has one condition...marriage!

#3259 UNCOVERING HER NINE MONTH SECRET

by Jennie Lucas

One glance from Alejandro, Duke of Alzacar, and I was his. Nine months on, he's found me again. But no matter how my body and my heart react to him, I'll *never* let him take our son away from me....

#3260 UNDONE BY THE SULTAN'S TOUCH

by Caitlin Crews

What would Khaled bin Aziz, Sultan of Jhurat, want with an ordinary girl like Cleo Churchill? She seems to be the convenient bride Khaled needs to unite his warring country, until their marriage unearths a passion that threatens to consume them both!

HPCNM0714RA

#3261 HIS FORBIDDEN DIAMOND

by Susan Stephens

Diamond dynasty heir Tyr Skavanga returns home haunted by the terrors of war. But one person defies his defenses...the exotically beautiful and strictly off-limits Princess Jasmina of Kareshi. With both their reputations at stake, can they resist their undeniable connection?

#3262 THE ARGENTINIAN'S DEMAND

by Cathy Williams

When Emily Edison resigns, her gorgeous billionaire boss, Leandro Perez, won't let her off easily. She'll pay the price—two weeks in paradise at his side! With her family's future at risk, Emily faces the ultimate choice—duty...or desire?

#3263 TAMING THE NOTORIOUS SICILIAN

The Irresistible Sicilians

by Michelle Smart

Francesco never thought he'd see Hannah Chapman again—a woman so pure and untouched has no place in his world. But a newly determined Hannah has one thing left on her to-do list. And only one gorgeous Sicilian can help her!

#3264 THE ULTIMATE SEDUCTION

The 21st Century Gentleman's Club

by Dani Collins

Behind her mask at Q Virtus's exclusive ball, Tiffany Davis reveals her true self—a powerful businesswoman with a proposal for Ryzard Vrbancic. He rejects the deal, but her ruthless determination makes him eager to seduce from her the one thing she's not offering....

SPECIAL EXCERPT FROM

Jennie Lucas takes you on a thrilling journey of secrets and scandal in her dazzling new first-person narrative. Read on for an exclusive extract from UNCOVERING HER NINE MONTH SECRET:

* * *

HIS expression shuttered, and his dark eyebrows came down into a scowl. "His surname, however..."

I sighed. "I thought you might want to change that. But don't worry." I gave an awkward smile. "I won't hold you to your marriage proposal."

His eyes were dark and intense. "What if I want you to hold me to it?"

My lips parted in shock.

"What?" I said faintly.

His dark eyes challenged mine. "What if I want you to marry me?"

"You don't want to get married. You went on and on about all the women who tried to drag you to the altar. I'm not one of them!"

"I know that now." Leaning his arm across the baby seat, he cupped my cheek. "But for our son's sake, I'm starting to think you and I should be...together."

"Why?"

"Why not?" He gave a sensual smile. "As you said, I already broke one rule. Why not break the other?"

"But what has changed?"

"I'm starting to think...perhaps I can trust you." His eyes met mine. "And I can't forget how it felt to have you in my bed."

Something changed in the air between us. Something primal, dangerous. I felt the warmth of his palm against my skin and held my breath. As the limo drove through the streets of London, memories crackled through me like fire.

I remembered the night we'd conceived Miguel, and all the other hot days of summer, when I'd surrendered to him, body and soul. I trembled, feeling him so close in the backseat of the limo, on the other side of our baby. Every inch of my skin suddenly remembered the hot stroke of Alejandro's fingertips. My mouth was tingling, aching....

"That's not a good reason to marry someone. Especially for you. If I said yes, you'd regret it. You'd blame me. Claim that I'd only done it to be a rich duchess."

He slowly shook his head. "I think," he said quietly, "you might be the one woman who truly doesn't care about that. And it would be best for our son. So what is your answer?"

* * *

What will Lena Carlisle do when pushed to her limits by the notorious Duke of Alzacar?

Find out in
UNCOVERING HER NINE MONTH SECRET
August 2014

HPEXP0714-1